Tom Jones

Henry Fielding

Retold by James Butler
Activities by Justin Rainey

Editors: Richard Elliott, Frances Evans
Design and art direction: Nadia Maestri
Computer graphics: Sara Blasigh
Illustrations: Ivan Canu
Picture research: Laura Lagomarsino

© 2003   Black Cat Publishing,
          an imprint of Cideb Editrice, Genoa, Canterbury

First edition: September 2003

Picture credits: Mary Evans Picture Library: 5, 111; Fitzwilliam Museum of Cambridge, UK/Bridgeman Art Library: 49; bfi Stills: 137.

We would be happy to receive your comments and suggestions, and give you any other information concerning our material.
Our e-mail and web site addresses are:
editorial@blackcat-cideb.com
www.blackcat-cideb.com
www.cideb.it

CISQ

CISQCERT

TEXTBOOKS AND
TEACHING MATERIALS
The quality of the publisher's
design, production and sales processes has
been certified to the standard of
UNI EN ISO 9001

ISBN 88-7754-996-3 Book
ISBN 88-7754-929-7 Book + CD

Printed in Italy by Litoprint, Genoa

CONTENTS

First Certificate in English
                          examination-style exercises

T: GRADE 7 Trinity-style exercises (Grade 7)

     This story is recorded in full.
                          These symbols indicate the beginning
                          and end of the extracts linked to the
                          listening activities.

Henry Fielding
by Samuel Freeman.

About the Author

Henry Fielding was the son of an army officer, and was born in Somerset in 1707. He was educated at Eton, [1] where he made many friends who later became influential in public life. At the age of nineteen he caused a scandal when he tried to elope [2] with a beautiful heiress, [3] but the attempt failed and he eventually settled in London.

Fielding was determined to make money as a dramatist, and he wrote more than twenty-five plays that were successfully performed between 1728 and 1737. Most of his plays consisted of farce and satire.

He married Charlotte Cradock in 1734, and she became the model for Sophia in *Tom Jones*. The marriage was a happy one.

1. **Eton** : expensive and prestigious boarding school for boys near London.
2. **elope** : run away to get married.
3. **heiress** : woman who has inherited a lot of money.

In 1736 Fielding took over the management of the New Theatre in London. He wrote savage political satires for the theatre which offended the government of the day. The government responded by introducing the Licensing Act of 1737 – a form of theatrical censorship. This effectively brought Fielding's theatrical career to an end.

Fielding now turned his attention to the law and to journalism. He studied to become a barrister, [1] and he contributed heavily to a satirical magazine, *The Champion*. He qualified as a barrister in 1740, but was now in poor health and his legal career suffered as a result.

In 1741 he turned to novel writing, his first effort being a satire on Richardson's novel *Pamela*, which had become very popular in London. Fielding's satire, *An Apology for the Life of Mrs Shamela Andrews*, was published in 1741. He followed this with *The Adventures of Joseph Andrews and His Friend, Mr Abraham Adams*, in 1742, and *The Life and Death of Jonathan Wild the Great*.

Fielding's wife Charlotte died in 1744, and he wrote very little over the next two years. It is thought that he began planning *The History of Tom Jones, a Foundling*, in 1746. He caused a scandal in 1747 when he married his wife's maid [2] and friend, Mary Daniel.

In 1748 Fielding undertook [3] a new career, thanks to the patronage of influential friends. He was appointed a Justice of the Peace [4] in the Westminster area of London. He began to attack the corruption and injustice of the legal system. His jurisdiction [5] soon spread [6] to the whole

1. **barrister** : lawyer who presents a case in court.
2. **maid** : female servant.
3. **undertook** : began.
4. **Justice of the Peace** : non lawyer who acts as a judge in local courts.
5. **jurisdiction** : the area of his legal authority.
6. **spread** : widened.

county of Middlesex. He and his half-brother, Sir John Fielding, worked tirelessly [1] together to improve the legal system and to break up organised crime in the London area.

Henry Fielding died in Lisbon in October 1754.

1 Complete the table by filling in the missing details about Fielding's life.

Personal details	Career
1707: born in Somerset	
1726:	
1734:	
	1736:
	1740:
	1741:
1744:	
1747:	
	1746:
	1748:
1754: died in Lisbon	

2 Which personal events in Fielding's life were the subject of scandal?

3 Which of the following careers did Fielding not have?

journalist/novelist/politician/theatre manager/musician/
Justice of the Peace/dramatist/barrister

1. **tirelessly** : with great energy.

Tom Jones

Mr Allworthy

Miss Bridget Allworthy
Mrs Blifil

Blifil

Mr Western

Sophia Western

Mrs Western

Molly Seagrim

Jenny Jones

Mrs Wilkins

Mr Partridge

Mrs Partridge

Lady Bellaston

Before you read

1 Fielding started to write *Tom Jones* in 1746. It is regarded as one of the great comic novels in English literature. Samuel Coleridge (1772-1834) regarded it also as one of the most perfect novels ever planned. **Before you read Chapter One, discuss with other students what the characteristics are of:**

a. *a comic novel.*
   The comic approach was very common in English literature in the 18th and early and mid 19th-century novel. Charles Dickens, for example, wrote about serious social questions (poverty, corruption, injustice) while at the same time creating comic personalities and situations;

b. *a well-planned novel.*
   Think of characters, time and place, for instance.

Think back at your ideas when you read the book.

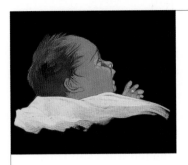

CHAPTER ONE

Mr Allworthy Finds a Baby

Mr Allworthy lived in Somerset. He was a gentleman, and a good, intelligent and kind man. He had married a very beautiful woman when he was young, and they had had three children, all of whom had died. His wife had also died. Mr Allworthy sometimes said that he still thought of himself as married – but that his wife had begun a journey without him.

Mr Allworthy lived with his sister Bridget. She was not beautiful or particularly good-natured, and she was over thirty years old. She often said that beauty was dangerous for a woman.

One night Mr Allworthy returned from London, where he had spent three months on business. He arrived very late and went straight to his bedroom after eating supper with Bridget. He was

Tom Jones

just about to climb into bed when he saw a small baby sleeping between the sheets. He was astonished at the sight, and rang the bell for his servant.

Mrs Deborah Wilkins was surprised to be called at such a late hour, and hurried to her master's room. When she saw the baby asleep on the bed, she too was astonished.

'What shall we do, sir?' she asked.

'Take care of the child this evening, Mrs Wilkins, and we'll find a nurse for it tomorrow morning,' Mr Allworthy ordered.

'I hope you'll find out who the mother is!' Mrs Wilkins said angrily. 'She should be punished for leaving a baby in someone else's house like that. It's as if she wanted people to believe you were the father, sir!'

'I'm sure she doesn't want to give that impression,' Mr Allworthy replied. 'I'm sure she just wants to make sure the child will be looked after properly.'

The next morning Mr Allworthy and Bridget were having breakfast together. Mr Allworthy asked Mrs Wilkins to bring in the child to show his sister. Bridget had very strong moral views, but she seemed sorry for the child. When her brother said that he had decided to adopt it, she agreed with him immediately that this was a good idea. She then spoke very bitterly against the wretched [1] mother, who she said deserved to be punished for her wickedness. [2]

Mrs Wilkins now tried to find out who the mother of the child was. She went into the village, where she knew all the families who had young daughters. There was one girl in particular, Jenny

---

1. **wretched** : unfortunate.
2. **wickedness** : bad behaviour.

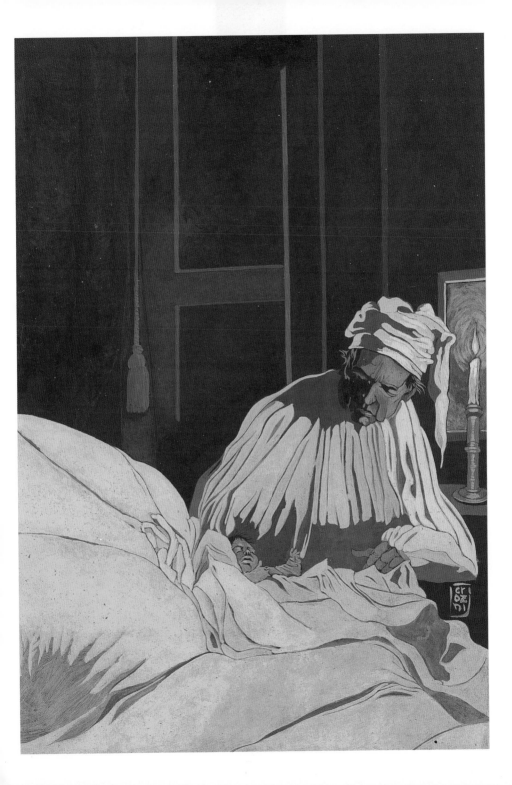

Tom Jones

Jones, whom she thought might be the mother of the child. Jenny Jones was not a very pretty girl, but she was very intelligent. She had lived for some years with the schoolmaster, Mr Partridge, and his wife. She got along very well [1] with Mr Partridge, who taught her Latin. She was so clever that she soon knew more than the schoolmaster himself. Mrs Partridge saw the friendship between her husband and the servant girl, and she was jealous of it. She made Jenny Jones leave the house. Her husband agreed to this, because the girl's cleverness humiliated him.

Mrs Wilkins was almost sure that Jenny Jones was the mother. Then she remembered that Jenny Jones had been to Mr Allworthy's house quite often recently, to look after Bridget when she was ill with a fever. She knew her way about [2] the house. She knew where the master's bedroom was!

Mrs Wilkins now hurried to Mr Allworthy to tell him her theory. He called Jenny Jones to the house, and spoke kindly to her. She admitted that she was the mother of the child, but she refused to say who the father was. Mr Allworthy admired her loyalty to the man who had seduced her. He promised to send her away from the village where she could begin a new life without dishonour to her name.

The mysterious baby was one delicate matter [3] in Mr Allworthy's house. There was another delicate matter as well. He had two friends who were brothers staying with him, one of whom was a doctor and the other a captain. Captain Blifil was about 35 years old, and he was a polite and educated man. He

---

1. **she ... well** : she had a good relationship.
2. **knew her way about** : was familiar with.
3. **delicate matter** : difficult situation.

studied Mr Allworthy's fine house and land, and thought that he could become rich by marrying Mr Allworthy's sister Bridget. He began to pay special attention to her, and they talked together about religion and other subjects. Soon they understood each other. They told everyone they wanted to get married. Mr Allworthy was delighted with the news, and congratulated the couple on their happiness.

Eight months after the wedding, Mrs Blifil gave birth to a son, Master Blifil. Mr Allworthy was delighted. He told Bridget that her son could be educated with the little foundling, [1] to whom he had given the name Tom Jones.

It was now that Mrs Wilkins made another discovery regarding the father of Tom Jones. Mrs Partridge had been jealous of the friendship between Jenny Jones and her husband. She had not really believed that her husband was unfaithful. Now, however, she began to hear the local gossip about Jenny Jones's baby. She also heard that Jenny Jones had gone away. Suddenly all of her jealousy came back to her, and she accused her husband of being unfaithful. He denied the charge, [2] and they argued violently. At last, for the sake of [3] peace with his wife who accused him constantly, Mr Partridge admitted that he was guilty.

News of the argument between the Partridges soon reached Mr Allworthy, and he was determined to interview the couple in order to discover the truth about Tom Jones. He ordered them to appear in front of him.

Mrs Partridge told the whole story to Mr Allworthy, and added

---

1. **foundling** : baby without parents.
2. **denied the charge** : said that it wasn't true.
3. **for the sake of** : in order to have.

that her husband had admitted his guilt to her in private. Mr Partridge said that he had not been Jenny Jones's lover. He said that he had only admitted being so in order to make peace with his wife who was jealous.

Mr Allworthy demanded that Mr Partridge admit his guilt, but the schoolmaster repeated that he was innocent. Mr Allworthy then told him that he was a guilty man and a liar. He said that he did not want to pay him the ten pounds a year as the local schoolmaster in the future.

The couple left Mr Allworthy's house very sad. They were now very poor, and Mr Partridge's school began to fail. His wife died soon after, and Mr Partridge himself left the area.

None of these events changed Mr Allworthy's affection for the young Tom Jones, who continued to be his favourite.

Meanwhile Captain Blifil spent a great deal of his time calculating how much money the Allworthy family had. He could not wait for Mr Allworthy to die.

He imagined himself spending his wife's money to improve the house and land. These pleasant fantasies came to a sudden end one day, however, when the captain was out taking his daily walk. He had a sudden attack and died of apoplexy. [1]

---

1. **apoplexy** : convulsion, a heart attack.

1 Look at these pictures. They illustrate domestic situations at the very beginning of the chapter.

The Allworthy House

Mr Allworthy

Mrs Deborah Wilkins

Miss Bridget Allworthy

The Partridge House

Mr Partridge

Mrs Partridge

Jenny Jones

a. In pairs, ask and answer questions about the people in the two houses. For example:

Who is Mr Allworthy? He's a gentleman from Somerset.
He is Bridget Allworthy's brother.

....

....

....

....

18

At the end of the chapter

The Allworthy House

Mr Allworthy

Master Blifil
and Mrs Blifil

Mrs Deborah Wilkins

b. What has happened by the end of the chapter in these houses? In pairs, ask and answer questions about what has changed.
For example: *What has happened to the Partridge family? Who is Mrs Blifil?*

c. Draw a picture showing the situation at the middle of the chapter (page 15, paragraph ending *... Mr Allworthy was delighted with the news, and congratulated the couple on their happiness.*).
Ask and answer questions similar to those you prepared in parts a. and b.

2 **Put these events from Chapter One into their correct order. There is one event that you will not use! The first event has been done for you.**

Event	Order
a. Mr Partridge insists he is not Tom Jones's father but Mr Allworthy refuses to believe him and stops paying him.	☐
b. Mrs Wilkins assumes that Jenny Jones is Tom's mother.	☐
c. Captain Blifil marries Miss Allworthy.	☐
d. Mr Allworthy finds a baby on his bed.	1
e. People in the village suspect Mr Partridge is Tom's father.	☐
f. Tom and Master Blifil have an argument.	☐
g. Mrs Blifil gives birth to a son.	☐
h. Mr Allworthy decides to adopt the foundling, Tom Jones.	☐
i. Captain Blifil dies.	☐
j. Mr Partridge leaves the area after the death of his wife.	☐

FCE **3** **For questions 1-10 choose from the characters introduced in Chapter One listed below (A-G). There is an example at the beginning (0). You can use a character more than once.**

A	Mr Allworthy	**E**	Jenny Jones
B	Miss Bridget Allworthy	**F**	Mr Partridge
C	Mrs Deborah Wilkins	**G**	Captain Blifil
D	Tom Jones		

Which character is described as

0. ☐A being a good man?

1. ☐ not liking beauty in a woman?

2. ☐ Mr Allworthy's favourite?

3. ☐ not being sympathetic to human error?

4. ☐ having made decisions based on money rather than love?

5. ☐ being very intelligent but not very pretty?

6. ☐ being a polite and educated man?

7. ☐ carrying out an investigation?

8. ☐ feeling humiliated by someone's progress?

9. ☐ admirably loyal?

10. ☐ determined to find out the truth about Tom Jones?

4 **The world Fielding described in 1749 was very different from today but human nature is the same. Which of these events in Chapter One listed below would be unusual today and which would not be. Discuss your ideas with your partner.**

Event	Unusual today?
a. Mr Allworthy lost all three of his children.	....
b. Jenny Jones abandoned her child.	....
c. Mr Allworthy adopted the foundling, Tom Jones.	....
d. Miss Bridget Allworthy was strongly critical of what she regarded as immoral behaviour.	....
e. There was a lot of gossip about Jenny Jones' baby.	....
f. Mr Allworthy sent Jenny Jones away from the village to give her the possibility of starting a new life.	....
g. Captain Blifil could not wait for Mr Allworthy to die so he could get his money.	....
h. Mr Allworthy interviewed Mr and Mrs Partridge in order to discover the truth about Tom Jones.	....

5 Check the meaning of the following verbs in an English learner's dictionary. Which one is different? Why?

> insult   make fun of someone   humiliate
> respect   criticise

Which verb best describes Fielding's attitude towards the following characters we met in Chapter One? Discuss your reasons with your partner.

- Mrs Blifil (Miss Bridget Allworthy)
- Mrs Deborah Wilkins
- Captain Blifil

Read the opening paragraph of Chapter One again.

(Mr Allworthy) **had married** *a very beautiful woman... and they* **had had** *three children...*

Most of the verbs are in the Past Perfect tense (had + past participle). This tense describes an action or state that occurred before another event in the past. The opening paragraph describes Mr Allworthy's life before the beginning of the story.

6 Complete the table below. An example has been done for you.

This event happened before...	this event
• (Mr Allworthy) **had married** a very beautiful woman... and they **had had** three children...	the beginning of the story
• Mr Allworthy had spent three months in London on business	
• Jenny Jones had lived with the Partridges	
• Jenny Jones had left the village	

Looking ahead

1 In exercise two on page 20 you had to put events from the opening chapter into their correct order. One event – f. *Tom and Master Blifil have an argument* – comes from Chapter Two 'Tom's Early Adventures', describing Tom's early life.

    a. **Which of the sentences below do you think could be the reason for the argument?**

        1. Blifil had made fun of Tom.

        2. Blifil had insulted Tom.

        3. Blifil had stolen something from Tom.

        4. Blifil had got Tom into trouble.

        5. Blifil and Tom argued about a girl.

    b. **Listen to the beginning of Chapter Two and check whether you were right.**

2 **Listen again. Some important new characters are introduced. Decide whether these statements are true or false. If it is true, tick A, if it is not true, tick B.**

	A	B
1. Mr Allworthy's neighbours preferred Tom to Master Blifil.	☐	☐
2. Mr Square and Mr Thwackum had similar opinions.	☐	☐
3. Seagrim agreed to go shooting for partridges with Tom.	☐	☐
4. Tom and Seagrim were both punished for shooting partridges on Squire Western's land.	☐	☐
5. Mr Thwackum punished Tom.	☐	☐

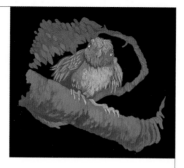

CHAPTER **TWO**

Tom's Early Adventures

Tom Jones and Master Blifil grew up together, and everybody commented on how very different they were from each other. Tom was high-spirited, [1] and was often in trouble for foolish pranks. [2] Master Blifil, on the other hand, was quiet and polite, and he seemed very religious. Most of the neighbours thought that Tom was badly behaved.

The boys had two tutors, Mr Square and Mr Thwackum. These two men did not agree about anything. Mr Square was a philosopher. He thought that human nature was perfect, and that wickedness was a deviation from natural perfection. Mr

---

1. **high-spirited** : full of energy and cheerfulness.
2. **pranks** : practical jokes.

Thwackum, on the other hand, believed that human nature was wicked because of the Fall. [1]

One incident in particular seemed to prove that Tom was a wicked boy. It happened when he was about fourteen years old. His best friend among the servants in Mr Allworthy's house was the gamekeeper, [2] George Seagrim. One day he persuaded the gamekeeper to go shooting with him. They went after some partridges [3] on Squire [4] Western's land, which was forbidden to them. Squire Western heard their gun go off, [5] and rode towards Tom and the gamekeeper. The gamekeeper managed to escape by hiding in a bush. The squire caught Tom, however, and took him home for punishment.

Mr Allworthy asked Tom if he had been alone on the squire's land, or if someone had come with him. Tom wanted to protect his friend, and so he insisted that he had been alone in the venture. The next morning Mr Thwackum gave the boy a severe beating.

The incident did not end there, because Tom and Master Blifil had an argument, during which Blifil called Tom a 'beggarly bastard'. [6] Tom hit him on the nose, and Blifil immediately ran to Mr Thwackum to complain. [7] When Tom was asked to explain what had happened, he repeated the insult that Blifil had used.

'It's not true, sir,' Blifil argued, 'but it's not surprising that

1. **the Fall** : story of Adam and Eve in the Bible.
2. **gamekeeper** : man whose job is to look after the birds and animals for shooting on a gentleman's estate.
3. **partridges** : short tailed game birds shot for sport.
4. **Squire** : titled land owner.
5. **go off** : fire.
6. **'beggarly bastard'** : without any money and without parents. A beggar is a mendicant.
7. **complain** : lament.

Tom Jones

END

Tom is lying. Somebody who lies once always lies again.'

'What do you mean?' Thwackum asked eagerly.

'Tom was lying when he said he was alone on Squire Western's land,' Blifil said. 'The gamekeeper Black George was with him.'

Both the tutors thought that Tom should be punished for lying and for hitting Blifil, but Mr Allworthy disagreed. He thought that Tom had behaved well to protect his friend the gamekeeper. He dismissed [1] the gamekeeper, however. He said that Black George had allowed Tom to be beaten instead of telling the truth himself.

When the story became known, most people thought Tom had behaved courageously. They agreed that Blifil was a sneak. [2] They criticised Mr Allworthy for dismissing George Seagrim.

Squire Western had a daughter, Sophia, who was regarded by everyone as a beauty. Being neighbours, Tom gave Sophia a little bird in a cage. Sophia loved the little bird and looked after it with great care. One day, when Mr Allworthy and his family were visiting the squire, Master Blifil asked to see the bird. He took it out of the cage and it immediately flew away into a tree. Sophia was very upset, and Tom climbed into the tree to take the bird back for her. Unfortunately, however, Tom fell out of the tree into the river below. Sophia thought he was hurt, and she began to call loudly for help. Tom was not seriously injured by his fall, but Sophia's bird flew away once more. A hawk [3] flew after it and killed it.

The years went by, and Tom grew into a good-looking young man. He always kept in close contact with the Seagrims. He felt

1. **dismissed** : ended the employment of.
2. **sneak** : someone who tells stories about other people.
3. **hawk** : bird of prey.

responsible for the family after the gamekeeper's dismissal from Mr Allworthy's service. He took his responsibility so seriously that he asked Squire Western's daughter, Sophia, to persuade her father to give Black George a job. The squire loved his daughter and he did as she asked him.

Mr Seagrim had a beautiful daughter, Molly, and she fell in love with Tom. At first the young man resisted her advances, but she was very insistent. She followed Tom wherever he went, and in the end she was successful. Tom and Molly had a short love affair, and the consequences of it were serious for Tom – Molly was now expecting a baby.

Molly's family were furious with her when the truth of her condition [1] became known, as she had just received a good offer of employment: Sophia had also noticed how attractive Molly Seagrim was and wanted the girl to work as her maid. However, Molly refused.

'I'm not going to wash dishes for anyone!' she told her father proudly. 'My gentleman will look after me very well. Look what he gave me this afternoon.' She pulled some money out of her pocket to show her father.

Now she turned to her mother.

'There'll be money for all of us if we're clever,' she said.

Her mother thought for a moment.

'Perhaps this job is not such a good one,' she said thoughtfully.

The family discussed the matter carefully, and they decided that Mrs Seagrim herself should work for Sophia Western as a maid, rather than Molly.

---

1. **condition** : (here) pregnancy.

The next day Tom was dining at Squire Western's house. Sophia was there, and she was in especially high spirits – perhaps because of Tom's presence at her house.

The local parson [1] Mr Supple was also a guest. He now began talking about Molly Seagrim.

'She's expecting a baby,' he told Squire Western. 'And she refuses to say who the father is. Squire Allworthy is going to send her to prison.'

At this news Tom jumped up from the table. He apologised for his behaviour, saying that he had just remembered some urgent business. Then he rushed [2] from the house.

'I see it all now,' Squire Western commented to the parson. 'Young Tom must be the father of Molly's baby. That's why he hurried off like that.'

'I don't want to think that about Tom,' the parson replied.

'What's to be sorry about?' Squire Western asked. 'Everybody has this kind of love affair – they're not so important.' Now he turned to Sophia. 'You agree with me, don't you, my dear?'

Sophia blushed. [3] She did not answer her father's question.

Tom meanwhile rushed off to rescue Molly. The constable [4] was taking her to prison. He told the officer to take her to Mr Allworthy's house instead.

'I'm the father of her child, sir,' he said to Mr Allworthy. 'Please do not send her to prison. It is my fault.'

Mr Allworthy told the constable to free the girl. He was very

1. **parson** : minister of the church.
2. **rushed** : went very quickly.
3. **blushed** : went red in the face.
4. **constable** : officer of the law, lowest rank of policeman.

Tom Jones

angry with Tom, but he was also pleased that the young man had admitted his fault so quickly. He began to understand that Tom's emotions could lead him astray, [1] but that he was an honest young man who told the truth.

Mr Thwackum and Mr Square, however, disliked Tom. They wanted to harm [2] him.

'Now I understand why Tom defended the gamekeeper,' Mr Square told Mr Allworthy. 'He protected the father so that he could seduce the daughter!'

Mr Square's accusation had a great influence on Allworthy's mind. It was the first bad impression he had received of Tom.

Mr Western was a very enthusiastic huntsman. He insisted that Sophia should come hunting with him, although Sophia did not enjoy the sport. One day they were out hunting when she lost control of her horse. She struggled [3] to control the animal, but she was in danger of falling. Tom saw what was happening and rushed up to her. He seized hold of [4] her horse's bridle. [5] The horse reared, [6] throwing Sophia off its back. Tom caught her in his arms. Sophia thanked him for what he had done.

'I'm glad you're safe,' Tom replied happily, 'even if I have hurt myself.'

'Hurt!' replied Sophia. 'How are you hurt?'

'Don't be worried,' Tom told her. 'It's nothing. I've broken my arm, that's all.'

---

1. **lead him astray** : make him do unwise things.
2. **harm** : injure.
3. **struggled** : fought with difficulty.
4. **seized hold of** : took with force and speed.
5. **bridle** : leather straps around a horse's head.
6. **reared** : rose onto its back legs.

Mr Western now joined Sophia and Tom, and they all went on foot to his house. The squire was very worried about his daughter, who looked pale and ill. She was worried about the injury to Tom.

Mr Western called a surgeon to treat the young man. The surgeon set [1] the arm and said he must go to bed and rest.

1. **set** : operation performed on a broken limb. The limb is placed in plaster so that it can not move.

Tom Jones

Sophia's maid, Mrs Honour, had been in the room when the surgeon was setting Tom's arm. She now went to her mistress and described how brave the young man had been during the painful operation.

'He's so good-looking, too!' Mrs Honour added.

'I believe you've fallen in love with him,' Sophia joked.

'And why shouldn't I fall in love with him?' Mrs Honour replied quickly. 'He's not really a gentleman – his parents were not married. Besides, the men in my family are too proud to have anything to do with Molly Seagrim!'

'Don't talk about one of my father's friends in that way!' Sophia said angrily. 'And never mention Molly Seagrim's name to me again!'

'I'm sorry I offended you,' she said. 'The truth is I do like Mr Jones. He likes you, too,' the maid went on. 'Once, when you were playing the harpsichord, Mr Jones was in the next room. He looked so sad that I asked him what he was thinking about. "I'm thinking about your mistress," he told me. "The man who marries her will be very lucky." That's what he told me.'

Sophia blushed very deeply.

1 In any story or narrative the reader develops a relationship with its characters. In children's stories for instance, we have heroes and villains. The reader's relationship with the characters in the story he/she is reading will be influenced strongly by the writer's presentation of the same character. We saw in Chapter One exercise five (page 22) how Fielding makes fun of some of his characters.

a. **What do you think Fielding feels towards Mr Allworthy and Captain Blifil? Use the text to justify your answer. Discuss your ideas with other students. How do you feel towards them?**

b. **Which of the characters listed below are presented positively and which are presented negatively?**

| Master Blifil   Molly Seagrim   Mr Square   Mr Thwackum |
| Sophia   The Seagrim family   Tom |

Positively presented	Negatively presented

c. **What did the negative characters do in this chapter for the reader not to like them? Complete the table.**

Negatively presented	Why?

d. **What do you notice about the <u>number</u> of characters that can be described as 'good'? Discuss your ideas with other students in a small group.**

e. **Now summarise the table in a short paragraph. Begin 'Several characters introduced in the second chapter make life difficult for Tom...'**

FCE 2 Chapter Two can be divided into 3 parts. Choose the appropriate title A-D which best summarises each part. There is a title you will not need to use.

A ☐ Thwackum is satisfied

B ☐ Blifil: different and dangerous

C ☐ Sophia reveals her feelings for Tom

D ☐ Tom admits his responsibility

How did you decide? What connections are there between the titles you chose and the three parts?

3 a. Which of these adjectives best describe Tom and Master Blifil? Discuss your choices with a partner.

cheerful   naughty   lively   religious   serious
friendly   mean   quiet

Tom	Master Blifil

We can compare Tom and Master Blifil by using the adjectives above in their comparative form.

b. Choose the correct comparative from the sentences below and then complete the rule.

• Master Blifil is *mean/more mean/meaner* than Tom.

• Tom is a *lively/more lively/livelier* child than Master Blifil.

• Master Blifil seems to be *religious/more religious/religiouser* than Tom.

c. **Now complete the rule.**

With one syllable adjectives (a)................;
with (b)................, change 'y' to 'i' and add -er;
with other adjectives of 2 or more syllables use (c)................ .

d. **Put the other adjectives into their correct form.**

FCE e. **Look at the table below. For questions 1-8 put the word given in capitals in its appropriate comparative form. There is an example at the beginning (0). One adjective will not be in a comparative form.**

The two children of the Allworthy house are very different. Although Master Blifil is (0)...*younger*... than Tom, he is (1)...................... and appears to the tutors Thwackum and Square to be (2)................... and probably (3)...................... .
In comparison to the late Captain Blifil's son, Tom is an (4)...................... child who enjoys outdoor activities. Master Blifil appears (5)...................... with books and study. Tom is described as being (6)...................... than Master Blifil as well as being a (7)...................... child. The reader can associate with Tom's foolish pranks; they are certainly (8)...................... than the seriousness of Master Blifil.

| YOUNG |
| SERIOUS |
| RESPECT |
| STUDY |
| ENERGY |
| HAPPY |
| HONEST |
| LIKE |
| NATURE |

4 *Tom's emotions could lead him astray, but... he was an honest young man who told the truth* (page 30). We get to know Tom and start to like him not only because of the good things he does but also through the mistakes he makes which highlight a 'good side' to his personality.

a. **What good things does Tom do in Chapter Two? Who is directly involved?**

....
....

b. **Complete the table**

Mistake	Good side revealed
• Tom takes George Seagrim shooting on Squire Western's land	• ....
•	• He admitted his involvement with Molly immediately so saving her from prison

5 **Authority**

Society was very different in Fielding's day in comparison to today. Which incident in Chapter Two highlights this?

Looking ahead

1 **Chapter Three is entitled 'Disaster Strikes Tom'.**
What do you think this disaster could be? Choose from the list below. Compare your choice with your partner.

a. he discovers Molly Seagrim with another man

b. he is discovered with another woman

c. he is discovered with Molly Seagrim

d. he is discovered with Molly and hits Blifil

e. he is hit by Thwackum

After you have read Chapter Three check to see if you were right.

CHAPTER **THREE**

Disaster Strikes Tom

om had many visitors while he was in bed at Mr Western's house. Mr Allworthy came often, and tried to persuade him to think seriously about his behaviour. He spoke kindly because he was fond of [1] the young man.

Thwackum also visited Tom, but he was very severe in his comments.

'Your broken arm is a judgement from God on your bad behaviour,' he told Tom.

Square was another visitor. According to his philosophy, the injury had no meaning at all.

Squire Western often came to the sickroom. He was grateful to

---

1. **was fond of** : liked.

Tom Jones

Tom for saving his daughter. Tom knew, however, that the squire wanted Sophia to marry a rich man. It seemed impossible that he could ever declare his love for her.

Tom now began to think about Molly. He had promised to be faithful to her, and he was a man of honour. He knew that she needed a man to protect her now that she was having a baby. At last an idea came to him. He decided to give her some money instead of marrying her.

When he was well enough to leave his bed, Tom went to Molly's house to talk to her. Her elder sister told him that the girl was in bed. He went upstairs to her room.

Molly seemed so pleased to see him that she was unable to speak for a few seconds. Tom began to explain that he could never marry her.

'Mr Allworthy has told me not to see you again,' he explained.

'You said you loved me,' the girl complained. 'Are you going to abandon me now that I'm in trouble? I shall never trust another man as long as I live!'

A little accident interrupted her speech. A rug [1] that was hanging on the wall fell down. Tom turned, and saw Mr Square hiding there. He understood immediately that Molly had another lover! The philosopher was embarrassed for a moment, then he stepped forward.

'You are amused to see me here,' he said to Tom, 'but you must remember one thing. I did not corrupt [2] this girl – you did that.'

I shall never tell anyone what you have done,' Tom replied, 'if

1. **rug** : small carpet.
2. **corrupt** : seduce.

you promise to be kind to her. And you, Molly,' he went on 'be faithful to your new friend.'

Tom left Molly and Square together and went downstairs. He was still worried that he was the father of Molly's child. One of her sisters now told him that he had not been Molly's first lover. He now felt that he had no further responsibility towards her.

Tom's thoughts now returned to Sophia. He tried his best to hide his love for her. He knew that Mr Western and Mr Allworthy did not consider him a possible suitor [1] for her. It was very difficult for him to avoid Sophia, however, as he continued to be Mr Western's guest.

One day he and Sophia met in the garden together.

'I'm so unhappy,' he told her suddenly.

He regretted what he had said immediately.

'I don't understand you,' Sophia replied.

'I don't want you to understand me,' he told her. 'Forgive me for what I said just now. I couldn't help it. I have tried not to speak about my love, but being alone with you here is too much for me!'

Sophia looked very seriously at him. She, too, was overcome [2] with love for him.

'I'm going into the house. If you love me,' she begged him, 'don't follow me.'

Mr Allworthy fell ill while Tom was staying at Mr Western's house, and his doctor told him he was dangerously ill. The good man was not frightened of death, and he sent for all the members of the household. Thwackum, Square, Blifil, Tom, and some of

1. **suitor** : potential fiancé.
2. **overcome** : full of.

the servants, gathered around the sick man's bed.

'I have sent for you all,' Mr Allworthy told them, 'because I want you to know what will happen after I die. You,' he said to Blifil, 'will inherit everything except for £500 pounds a year which I leave to you, Tom. I am also leaving you £1,000 pounds in cash.'

Tom took hold of Mr Allworthy's hand. He told him he could not express his gratitude for Mr Allworthy's kindness to him. He began to cry while he was speaking.

'I know you have a lot of goodness and generosity in you,' Mr Allworthy told him kindly.

Now Mr Allworthy spoke to Thwackum and Square.

'I have left you £1,000, each,' he told them.

A servant entered the room saying that a lawyer had arrived from London with an important message. Mr Allworthy sent Blifil to see what it was all about. Mr Allworthy was now very tired and he fell asleep.

A few minutes later Blifil came back into the room. His expression was very serious. He told everyone that his mother had died. They agreed to tell Mr Allworthy the news if the doctor thought he was strong enough.

Some time later Mr Allworthy woke up. The doctor examined the patient carefully, and announced that he was now out of danger.

Mr Allworthy asked what the lawyer had had to say, and was sad to hear of his sister's death. He wanted to speak to the lawyer himself, but Blifil said he had already left the house on other urgent business.

Tom was delighted that Mr Allworthy was recovering from his illness. He drank far too much wine that evening. He became very

41

Tom Jones

drunk and cheerful. He went outside into the garden to cool his head, and there he saw Molly Seagrim. Tom was a young man, and he was drunk; Molly was a young woman and she was beautiful. They talked together for a while, and then they looked around the garden for a quiet place where they could be alone together.

It happened that Blifil and Thwackum were also in the garden that evening, and they saw Tom and Molly.

'I wonder who they are!' Blifil said.

Blifil and Thwackum went after the couple. They made so much noise that Tom heard them. He came forward out of the darkness.

'Is that you, Tom?' Thwackum asked. 'And who's the woman with you?'

'I won't tell you,' Tom answered firmly. [1]

'Then I'll find out!' Thwackum cried angrily.

'No, you won't!' cried Tom. He was determined to protect Molly.

Thwackum and Tom now began struggling together fiercely. Blifil joined in the fight, but he was soon punched [2] to the ground by Tom. After a while, however, Thwackum and Blifil overpowered [3] Tom, whose arm was still in a bandage.

Now Mr Western joined the fight. He had been out riding with the parson, Sophia's aunt, and Sophia. He heard the shouts and cries of the adversaries, and saw that two men were fighting against one man. He ran forward to help. Together Mr Western

---

1. **firmly** : defiantly.
2. **punched** : hit with the hand.
3. **overpowered** : defeated.

and Tom quickly defeated Thwackum and Blifil.

The parson and the two women now arrived. They saw Tom covered in blood and Blifil lying on the ground. They saw Thwackum, who also had blood on him, and they saw Mr Western. He was very proud of his part in the struggle.

Blifil lay on the ground without moving, and everyone began to worry that he was dead. They moved towards him, when suddenly Sophia gave a cry and fell to the ground. She had fainted [1] with shock.

'Sophia's dead!' Mrs Western screamed.

Tom rushed over to Sophia. He picked her up and carried her to a river that was close by. He washed her face gently with water, and after a few moments she regained consciousness. [2]

Mr Western thanked Tom for saving his daughter's life. He had found out by now what the fight was about, and he thought it was very funny.

'Fighting over a woman, were you?' he teased [3] Tom.

1. **fainted** : lost consciousness.
2. **regained consciousness** : woke up.
3. **teased** : made fun of, mocked lightly in a friendly manner.

1 **Answer these questions.**

    a. Which event listed in looking ahead exercise one (page 23), Chapter Two, was the disaster?

    b. Which event did NOT take place?

    c. Three of the remaining events listed took place. Which are they?

FCE 2 **Choose the best answer (A, B, C or D) which you think fits best according to Chapter Three. There is an example (0) at the beginning.**

    0. Which of Tom's visitors did he probably look forward to seeing while in his sickroom?

      A ☐ Molly Seagrim

      B ☐ Thwackum

      C ☐ Square

      D ☑ Mr Allworthy and Squire Western

    1. Tom decided to help Molly by

      A ☐ leaving the area

      B ☐ giving her money

      C ☐ marrying her

      D ☐ introducing her to Mr Square

    2. Which sentence best describes Tom's feelings as he left Molly's house?

      A ☐ he is upset that Molly has another man

      B ☐ he is pleased he can embarrass Mr Square

      C ☐ he feels he no longer has to help Molly

      D ☐ he wants to speak to Molly's father

    3. Apart from being in love, which word best describes Tom's feelings for Sophia?

      A ☐ respectful

      B ☐ irritated

      C ☐ impatient

      D ☐ understanding

4. Where was Tom when Mr Allworthy became ill?

   A ☐ London

   B ☐ on his way to London

   C ☐ at Squire Western's

   D ☐ somewhere else

5. What event happened first?

   A ☐ Mr Allworthy told his household how he would distribute his property

   B ☐ a lawyer arrived from London

   C ☐ Blifil was told that his mother had died

   D ☐ Blifil's mother died

6. Why did Tom celebrate?

   A ☐ he was happy about the fortune he had inherited

   B ☐ he was glad Blifil's mother had died

   C ☐ he was happy to be near Sophia again

   D ☐ he was happy that Mr Allworthy was no longer in danger

7. Which of the following statements is NOT true?

   A ☐ Tom seduced Molly against her wishes

   B ☐ Blifil and Thwackum saw Molly and Tom

   C ☐ Thwackum wanted to know who Tom was with

   D ☐ Tom provoked Thwackum into a fight

8. Why did Squire Western join in the fight?

   A ☐ he had always disliked Blifil

   B ☐ he thought two against one was not fair

   C ☐ he wanted to show Sophia he was still a strong man

   D ☐ the parson had told him to help Tom

9. How many people were present at the end of the fight?

   A ☐ seven

   B ☐ six

   C ☐ five

   D ☐ four

10. How did Tom help Sophia?

A ☐ he told the parson to fetch help

B ☐ he told Squire Western that his daughter was unwell

C ☐ he brought her water from the river

D ☐ he helped her regain consciousness

3 **Choose from the sentences A-H the one which fits each group (1-6). There is an extra sentence which you do not need to use. There is an example (0) at the beginning.**

> My dearest brother,
>
> You may think life here in deepest Somerset for a village parson is a boring existence.
>
> Possibly life in the metropolis is full of excitement. However, (0)........C.......
>
> The area has some fine houses, notably those of a Mr Allworthy and a Squire Western. (1)............... . He is an amusing and generous host. He has a charming daughter, Sophia, who is judged rightly by all to be a beauty.
>
> The Squire has a young friend who is also a frequent guest of his house. (2)............... . The boy is handsome and courteous and, it appears, much liked by the women.
>
> Two extraordinary events have marked my stay with the Squire and both involve young Jones.
>
> One evening at dinner with the Squire, his daughter and Mr Jones, I informed my host that a local girl, a certain Molly Seagrim, was expecting a child and refused to reveal the father's name to Mr Allworthy.
>
> (3)............... . At that moment Mr Jones stood up and, apologising, left the table in a great hurry. The Squire was convinced that Tom was the father.
>
> Some time later a party made up by myself, the Squire and Sophia was out riding in the Squire's grounds.
>
> After a while, the Squire heard the shouts and cries typical of a fight. (4)............... .
>
> Our friend Tom Jones was outnumbered in a struggle with two men

> *(I will not test your patience with the details) and the Squire gave him assistance.*
> *Tom and the Squire had the best. It seems the two men, Mr Allworthy's nephew and his tutor, had discovered Jones in a moment of intimacy with a young woman. (5)............... . The very same Molly Seagrim I had given news of at the dinner table!*
> *(6)............. Blood and bodies, my dear brother, and what is more a lady in distress: Miss Sophia fainted!*
> *I fear Jones' strong emotions will lead him into trouble.*
> *I await your news, dear brother.*
> *My best regards,*

A Who was she?

B He rode ahead to see what was happening.

C I can assure you that this corner of England has its share of surprises.

D His name is Tom Jones, a foundling adopted by Mr Allworthy.

E I told them of Mr Allworthy's intention to send the unfortunate woman to prison.

F They had no embarrassment.

G I am often invited to dine at Squire Western's.

H What a scene!

4 In Chapter Two exercise five (page 36) you were asked to consider Mr Allworthy's authority in the local community. What other example is there in Chapter Three?

5 Answer these questions.

  a. How does Squire Western comment on the 'two extraordinary events' described in the parson's letter? (exercise three).

  b. What do these comments tell you about him?
  Do you think the Squire would accept a 'love affair' between his daughter and Tom? Discuss both questions in a small group.

The Early 18th-century Novel

(1) The demand for entertaining literature grew in the 18th century as a result of the industrial revolution that was transforming both the country's economy and its desire for entertainment of different kinds. More and more people were now able to read, and the market responded by providing exciting and accessible works.

(2) Although other authors had written long stories in prose before the 18th century, there is general agreement among critics that the English novel begins with Daniel Defoe's publication of *The Life and Strange Surprising Adventures of Robinson Crusoe* in 1719. The book, more commonly known as *Robinson Crusoe*, tells how the hero manages to survive on a deserted island. When Crusoe discovers that the island is not completely deserted, he takes charge. [1] Throughout the novel Crusoe uses reason and common sense to guide his behaviour, and there is a strong moral element in the narrative. Defoe wrote other novels, most notably *The Fortunes and Misfortunes of Moll Flanders*, 1722 and *Roxana*, 1724.

(3) Two novelists dominated the 1740's: Samuel Richardson and Henry Fielding. Richardson had been a printer and publisher who had written manuals of ethics for the new social classes that were coming into existence as a result of economic advances. His first

---

1. **charge** : command.

Pamela and Mr B. in the Summer House (*c.* 1744) by Joseph Highmore.

novel, *Pamela*; *or Virtue Rewarded*, 1740, is written in the form of letters. It tells the story of the heroine's persecution and attempted seduction by a gentleman, Mr B. Pamela retains her honour despite terrible sufferings, and in the end she is rewarded by marriage with her persecutor. The novel has a very strong moral tone, and was hugely successful with readers. Richardson's

masterpiece is *Clarissa; or, The History of a Young Lady*, 1747-8, which again tells the story of a man's pursuit and brutal treatment of a girl.

(4) Henry Fielding admired Richardson's *Clarissa*, but he wrote two novels that mock [1] the moral seriousness of *Pamela*. Fielding's *An Apology for the Life of Mrs Shamela Andrews*, 1741, retains the narrative and characters of Richardson's novel, but changes the heroine from a highly moral girl who accepts suffering into an egoistic girl who uses the language of morality to serve her own ends. [2] Fielding attacked *Pamela* again with his novel *The Adventures of Joseph Andrews and His Friend, Mr Abraham Adams*, 1742. Although the novel begins as parody, it introduces elements that are crucial to the development of the genre. Firstly, it abandons the letter form and makes use of third-person narrative. Secondly, Fielding describes it as a 'comic romance' where the comedy takes the form of mocking human affectation. [3] According to Fielding, affectation is the result of vanity or hypocrisy. Fielding comments that this is 'a kind of writing, which I do not remember to have seen attempted in our language'.

(5) Fielding produced another novel of a similar type, *The Life and Death of Jonathan Wild the Great*, 1743. The historical Jonathan Wild was a notorious [4] criminal who ended his life on the gallows. [5] In Fielding's novel, however, he is a 'great man' who succeeds because of his greed and cruelty.

1. **mock** : make fun of.
2. **serve her own ends** : for her own benefit.
3. **affectation** : false behaviour.
4. **notorious** : famously wicked.
5. **gallows** : wooden structure from which criminals were hung.

(6) Although many contemporaries criticised *Tom Jones* on moral grounds, critics nowadays regard the novel as very influential in the development of the genre. Fielding's writing makes use of several techniques that later writers also used with success. He has a 'mock heroic' style which emphasises the difference between how his characters really are, and how they would like to appear to the world or to themselves. He also makes wide use of the picaresque tradition. [1] His characters are frequently on the move around the country, and this allows the novelist to describe a wide range of people and social classes.

FCE **1** **The text has six paragraphs. Each paragraph can be summarised with a short title. Match the titles listed below (A-G) to the correct paragraph (1-6). There is one title you will not need.**

A ☐ The innovation of Fielding's prose

B ☐ Supply and demand

C ☐ Fielding the crime fighter

D ☐ Jonathan Wild: anti-hero

E ☐ Defoe and the origins of the novel

F ☐ *Tom Jones*: a mixture of styles

G ☐ The legacy of Richardson

1. **picaresque tradition** : style of Spanish writing detailing the comic misfortunes of someone living on the road.

2 Match the appropriate question (a, b or c) to the answer. An example (0) has been done for you.

0. Because more and more people were able to read.

    a. ☐ How did the publishing market respond to increased literacy?

    b. ☑ Why was there growth in the offer of books and magazines?

    c. ☐ What type of reading matter was particularly popular?

1. They were characterised by a strong moral tone.

    a. ☐ Why are Defoe's works considered as the starting point of the English novel?

    b. ☐ What were the typical subject matters of the 18th-century novel?

    c. ☐ What did Defoe's and Richardson's works have in common?

2. He didn't like its moral seriousness.

    a. ☐ Why did Fielding write *Mrs Shamela Andrews*?

    b. ☐ What was Fielding's opinion of Richardson's *Pamela*?

    c. ☐ What was Richardson's opinion of *Mrs Shamela Andrews*?

3. It used third-person narrative.

    a. ☐ What was *Joseph Andrews* about?

    b. ☐ Why did Fielding regard his novel *Joseph Andrews* as innovative?

    c. ☐ What did he criticise in Richardson's *Pamela*?

4. Characters are frequently on the move and have several adventures.

    a. ☐ What is a characteristic of the picaresque tradition?

    b. ☐ What is a characteristic of the mock-heroic style?

    c. ☐ What is a characteristic of the comic romance?

FCE 3 For questions 1-18 read the text below and look carefully at each line. Some of the lines are correct, and some have a word which should not be there. If a line is correct put a tick (✔) by the number. If a line has a word which should not be there write the word in the right-hand column. There are two examples at the beginning (0) and (00).

THE LICENCING ACT 1737

0.	Theatre companies had been long needed a licence to present	*been*
00.	dramas. In Fielding's time two theatres were licensed to	✔
1.	perform plays – Covent Garden and Drury Lane, the 'patent	....
2.	theatres'. This strict system was formalised in the 1737 to	....
3.	counter the satirical plays, particularly those of Henry	....
4.	Fielding himself. The Licensing Act of 1737 confirmed the	....
5.	two theatres had already mentioned as the only venues	....
6.	licensed to perform plays. It also put up all plays under the	....
7.	control and supervision of the Lord Chamberlain.	....
8.	Theatrical bill inspectors went round to checking that the law	....
9.	was not being broken. They were employed either by the	....
10.	Lord Chamberlain's office and or by the patent theatres	....
11.	checking up on possibly illegal competition. The non-patent	....
12.	theatres filled their stages with harmless entertainments and	....
13.	theatre managers invented all ways of getting round the law	....
14.	by adding the music and charging admission for that.	....
15.	The Licensing Act had the most profound influence on	....
16.	English literature of any legislation in the past three	....
17.	centuries. It was created a low period in the history of the	....
18.	theatre which has lasted for a century. Serious writers came	....
19.	to disregard the theatre as a vehicle for serious thought –	....
20.	writers could not see their plays performed as written. This	....
21.	fact along with the rise of more literacy and new technology	....
22.	aided the development of the novel, a literary form Fielding	....
23.	turned to with success, in particular with *Tom Jones*.	....

Looking ahead

1 a. **Chapter Three was entitled 'Disaster Strikes Tom'. In the next chapter 'Mr Western Commands a Marriage' what do you think could be the worst thing to happen to Tom?**
Discuss your ideas with your partner.

b. **Now listen to the very beginning of Chapter Four and complete the following sentences:**

1. Sophia knew she was in love with Tom but ....
....

2. Mrs Western realised something was wrong with Sophia and she ....
....

3. Mr Western did not want Sophia to love ....
....

4. Mrs Western thought Sophia ....
....

5. Mr Western was happy about the news because ....
....

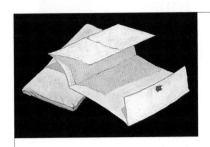

CHAPTER **FOUR**

Mr Western Commands a Marriage

Sophia was now aware that she was in love with Tom. She was determined to hide the fact from everybody. She could not hide her thoughtfulness, however, and her aunt began to wonder what was wrong with her. She discussed the question with Mr Western.

'She might be ill!' Mr Western said. 'We must send for a doctor.'

'I don't think she's ill,' Mrs Western replied with a little smile. 'I think she's in love.'

'Love!' shouted Mr Western. 'I won't let her be in love with anyone I disapprove of.'

Tom Jones

'You remember how she fainted when Mr Blifil was lying on the ground?' Mrs Western asked. 'I think she's in love with him.'

Mr Western thought for a moment. Then he smiled delightedly.

'Blifil, eh? But that's excellent news. Our estates [1] are side by side. What a perfect match!' [2]

END

Mrs Western said that the squire should suggest the marriage to Mr Allworthy. He readily agreed to this, and invited Mr Allworthy and his family to dinner.

Sophia was very careful during the dinner to hide her real feelings for Tom, and she paid particular attention to Blifil. Her aunt observed her carefully, and was more convinced than ever that her niece was in love with Blifil.

Mr Western had a private talk with Mr Allworthy after dinner. He suggested that the marriage would be a good idea. Mr Allworthy said that he would agree to it if the young couple loved each other.

When he arrived home, Mr Allworthy told Blifil of Mr Western's proposal. Blifil agreed to marry Sophia. Mr Allworthy then wrote to the squire saying that Blifil accepted the proposal.

Meanwhile Mrs Western was trying to discover Sophia's feelings for Blifil.

'You can't keep a secret from us,' she said encouragingly.

Sophia went red.

'What secret, aunt?' she asked.

'I saw how you behaved the other day,' her aunt went on. 'Your father and I have discussed the whole matter, and we

---

1.   **estates** : large areas of land with a house in the country.

2.   **match** : (here), marriage.

approve of your choice. Your lover is coming to see you later this afternoon.'

'This afternoon!' cried Sophia in astonishment.

'Yes, my dear. And it's me you should be grateful to. I know why you fainted, and I saw how you behaved at dinner. I told your father everything, and he has already proposed the marriage to Mr Allworthy. Mr Allworthy has agreed to it. That's why your lover is coming here this afternoon. He's a fine young man.'

'You're right,' said Sophia. 'And he's so brave and kind, as well. It's a pity he's so poor.'

'Mr Blifil's not poor,' her aunt said.

'Mr Blifil?' repeated Sophia in surprise. 'I was talking about Mr Jones.'

'Jones!' Mrs Western said scornfully. [1] 'You don't mean you're in love with him? You can't think of him. What a disgrace to the whole Western family!'

Sophia burst into tears, [2] but Mrs Western was still very angry with her. She threatened to tell Sophia's father what she had learned, but Sophia persuaded her to keep the secret. In return, Sophia agreed to meet Blifil when he came to the house later that afternoon.

The meeting with Blifil was awkward [3] because Sophia did not know what to say to him. He, however, merely assumed that she was very shy, and he was content.

When Blifil's visit was over, Mr Western told Sophia that he was very pleased with her. He said that she could buy whatever

1. **scornfully** : with disgust.
2. **burst into tears** : suddenly began to cry.
3. **awkward** : uncomfortable.

she wanted for the wedding.

Sophia thought she could take advantage of her father's loving mood to tell him the truth.

'I can't marry Mr Blifil,' she confessed.

'Can't!' cried her father angrily. 'Marriage doesn't kill anyone. Don't be so foolish!'

Sophia began to sob [1] painfully.

'You're going to marry him!' her father shouted. 'And if you don't do what I tell you, you won't have a penny.'

He pushed her violently away from him and ran out of the room. He saw Tom in the hall, and asked him to go in to Sophia.

Tom went to Sophia. He saw that she had been crying.

'I'm never going to marry Mr Blifil,' Sophia told him.

'Tell me there is some hope for me,' Tom begged [2] her.

'Hope?' cried Sophia desperately. 'I can't make my father unhappy.'

Suddenly Sophia and Tom heard Mr Western shouting furiously in another part of the house. He had just been listening to the truth about his daughter's love from Mrs Western.

A moment later Mr Western burst into the room [3] where the two lovers were. He was still furious, and he swore [4] at both Sophia and Tom. He wanted to fight Tom, but the young man refused.

'I won't hurt Sophia's father,' he said quietly.

The squire came to complain to Mr Allworthy the next day.

1. **sob** : cry.
2. **begged** : implored.
3. **burst into the room** : came noisily and quickly into the room.
4. **swore** : used bad or rude language.

Tom Jones

'My daughter's in love with your bastard,' he said. 'I won't give her a penny if she doesn't do what I want. But she will do what I want in the end – I promise you that!'

Blifil overheard [1] the conversation between the squire and Mr Allworthy. He now told his uncle about the fight he and Mr Thwackum had had with Tom.

'Tom was with a woman, you see,' he explained.

'My dear boy, you should have told me all this much sooner,' Mr Allworthy said.

The good man was very sad to learn about the fight, and he was determined to have a serious talk with Tom. That evening he told him that his behaviour had been so bad he must leave the house forever. He gave Tom £500 and sent him away.

Tom walked slowly away from the house that had been his home. He stopped by a little river to write a quick letter to Sophia. He was so sad that he left all his things on the ground when he started walking again. As he hurried back to collect them, he met his old friend, Black George. They went back together to look for Tom's things, but there was nothing there. Black George had passed that way earlier, and had stolen them.

Tom asked the gamekeeper to deliver his letter to Sophia. The gamekeeper agreed to do this.

---

1. **overheard** : heard unintentionally.

1 **a.** In Chapter Four Tom suffers three major misfortunes. What are they? Who is responsible for each one?

Misfortune	Person responsible
1.	
2.	
3.	

b. Match the definition (a, b, c) to these nouns:

> **1** a thief   **2** a misunderstanding   **3** a sneak

a ☐ an event when a person or people think they have understood someone or something but they have not

b ☐ someone who gets people into trouble by telling someone, generally in authority such as a teacher, that another person has done something bad

c ☐ a person who steals

c. Now match the nouns (1-3) to the three people you identified in 1a. In pairs, explain how each person was responsible for Tom's misfortunes

2 **a.** We saw in exercise one that Mrs Western 'misunderstands' Sophia's feelings. This mistake starts a 'train of events' that leads to the misfortune that Sophia experiences in Chapter Four. Complete the events below. The second has been done for you.

Mrs Western thinks Sophia
is in love with Master Blifil →

    1. .... →

        2. Squire Western tells Mr Allworthy →

            3. .... →

                4. Master Blifil agrees to marry Sophia

b. Misunderstandings are a classic comic device. In Chapter Four there is a moment when Mrs Western and Sophia are both victims of a misunderstanding.

And he's so brave and kind, as well [says Sophia] (page 57)

Who is 'he'?

   1. For Sophia, it's ...

   2. For Mrs Western, it's ...

c. When does the misunderstanding end?

3 Squire Western is not so easy-going as he appeared in the previous chapters (Chapter Three, exercise five, page 47) about his daughter and her feelings for Tom.

Which of the following statements about Squire Western do you agree with? Discuss your ideas with your partner.

		Agree	Don't Agree
a.	he wants his daughter to marry for love	☐	☐
b.	he cannot accept his daughter's marriage to a foundling	☐	☐
c.	the social and economic advantages of a good marriage are more important than love	☐	☐
d.	Western is selfish and thinks only of himself	☐	☐
e.	Western is worried about the fact his daughter does not love Blifil	☐	☐
f.	Western loves his daughter	☐	☐

T: GRADE 7

4 **a. Topic – The Family**

The Westerns and the Allworthys are not completely unlike families today. The following family relations exist in the two families.

father   aunt   sister   son   uncle   daughter

Complete the table below. An example has been done for you.

Relation	
• father	Squire Western is Sophia's father
• aunt	
• son	
• uncle	
• sister	
• daughter	

T: GRADE 7

b. **Draw your family tree**
    You are going to describe your family. Before you do, consider not only appearances but also personality, interests, etc. Make comparisons between them.
    Useful language:

- Appearance: *I look like my brother...; my father in his mid-forties; he's overweight; she's slim; she's got shoulder-length hair...*
- Personality; interests: *My sister takes after our mother, they are both musical. He really likes...*
- Comparison: *My father is not as easy-going as my mum; he's stricter than her...*
- Have you got a favourite relative (e.g. an uncle, aunt, etc.)?
- Squire Western appears to be the boss in his family. Who is 'the boss' in your family?

5 Chapter Four contains several reporting verbs: verbs that say HOW something was said and/or the PURPOSE.

- 'Please open the window!' **he asked.**
  Compare this with:
- 'Please open the window!' **he pleaded.**
- 'Please open the window!' **he demanded.**

The speaker's WAY of speaking and PURPOSE of speaking are different.

a. Which reporting verbs are used in Chapter Four? Make a list. Reporting verbs are also used in reported speech, but it is important to know what type of construction the verb needs, Look at the following in reported speech.

- He asked <u>him/her to open</u> the window.
- He pleaded <u>with him/her to open</u> the window.
- He demanded <u>that the window be opened/they opened</u> the window.

You can find the construction required by a reporting verb in an English learner's dictionary

FCE

b. For questions 1-5, complete the second sentence so that it has a similar meaning to the first sentence, using the word given. Do not change the word given. You must use between two and five words, including the word given. There is an example at the beginning (0).

0. 'I think you should write to Allworthy,' Mrs Western said to her brother.
   recommended
   Mrs Western ....<u>recommended writing to</u>........ Mr Allworthy.

1. 'Don't tell father, please,' Sophia asked her aunt.
   persuaded
   Sophia .... to tell her father.

2. 'Yes, it is true I do love Tom Jones,' Sophia said.
   confess
   Sophia .... loving Tom Jones.

3. 'I won't give her a penny if she doesn't do what I want,' Squire Western told Mr Allworthy.
   promise
   Squire ....his daughter a penny if she didn't do what he wanted.

4. 'Father don't make me marry Blifil,' Sophia told her father.
   beg
   Sophia .... to make her marry Blifil.

5. 'If I must then I will meet Blifil,' Sophia told her aunt, Miss Western.
   agree
   Sophia .... meet Blifil.

FCE 6 You are carrying out research into 'The daily life of your town in the mid 1700s'. Your school has decided to invite a local expert to give a talk to the students of your class.
You have made these notes about the letter you will write.

- invite him/her to give a talk
- the specific subject of her talk?
- any presentation aids (computer, projector, etc.)?
- we want to organise the talk at the end of next month
- appreciate quick reply!

Write a letter of between 120 and 180 words in an appropriate style. Start your letter like this:

Dear Mrs Blake,

My class is doing a project on daily life in our town in the mid 18th century. Our teacher has told us that you are an expert in this field.

Looking ahead

1 Chapter Five is entitled 'On the Road'. We know that at the end of Chapter Four, Tom is on the road. Listen to this extract from the beginning of Chapter Five. Who else will be on the road and why?

1 For questions 1 to 35 read the text below and look carefully at each line. Five of the lines are correct while the other fifteen have a word which should not be there. If a line is correct put a tick (✓) by the line number. If a line has a word which should not be there, write it by the line number. There are two examples (0 and 00).

HIGHWAYMAN

A thief on horseback who robbed travellers on the highway (those who did so on foot were known as footpads).

0.	With the development of regular passing coach	*passing*
00.	services in the 17th and 18th centuries, highwaymen	✔
1.	became legendary and romantic figures. In an age	....
2.	where travel was already absolutely hazardous due to	....
3.	the lack of decent roads, no one rode alone without	....
4.	fear of being robbed, and people often joined company	....
5.	or hired escorts. Some of travellers often wrote their	....
6.	wills before they set out!	....
7.	One of the most dangerous areas than for travellers	....
8.	was Hounslow Heath to the west of London. Today it	....
9.	is now very largely buried beneath the runways of	....
10.	London Airport. Between the 17th and early 19th	....
11.	centuries, the Heath has occupied perhaps 25 square	....
12.	miles. No one was really certain where its boundaries	....
13.	lay, and no one who cared, for it was an area to be	....
14.	crossed as quickly as possible. Though Hounslow	....
15.	itself was not large, it was after London the most	....
16.	important of coaching centres. Across it the Heath ran	....
17.	the Bath Road and the Exeter Road, along much which	....
18.	travelled wealthy visitors to West Country resorts and	....
19.	courtiers travelling to the castle of Windsor.	....
20.	Perhaps because they were concentrated on the	....
21.	wealthy, the highwaymen became popular heroes.	....
22.	While many of the highwaymen were so often	....
23.	violent criminals, it cannot be denied that some of	....
24.	them had a certain flair. There are stories of some	....
25.	highwaymen who had returned money to some	....
26.	unfortunate, and released women and children	....

27. unharmed. Dick Turpin is probably the most ....
28. famous highwayman of all. His reputation even ....
29. today is of a person daring and dashing ....
30. highwayman who famously rode from London to ....
31. York on his faithful mare, Black Bess, in less than ....
32. the 24 hours. However, the popular Turpin legend ....
33. contains little more truth. He was in reality a ....
34. violent criminal who was responsible for some ....
35. hundreds of robberies. ....

2 Using the Internet find out about:

- Stagecoaches.
- Highwaymen: criminals that robbed stage coach passengers such as Dick Turpin.

Working in groups, prepare a class project on the two topics.

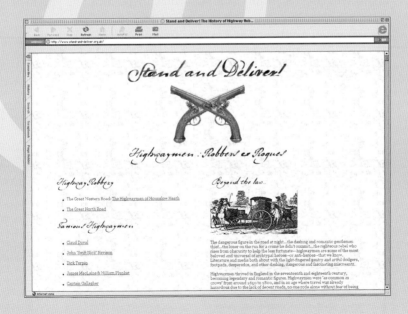

3 Henry Fielding, John Gay and William Hogarth

The three are widely accepted as major figures in English cultural life of the 18th century.
- Henry Fielding (1707-1754): novelist, journalist and theatre impresario.
- John Gay (1685-1732): poet and playwright.
- William Hogarth (1697-1764): artist.

The three were contemporaries. Through different art forms they provide us with a wonderful insight into 18th-century English life and society. We know something about Henry Fielding. Now let's find out more about John Gay and William Hogarth.

John Gay

John Gay's reputation has survived the passing of time principally thanks to one work: *The Beggar's Opera*, which he completed in 1728. It is a story about heroes, villains, love, confusion, sacrifice, betrayal, redemption and humour. Seventeen scenes in three acts span the course of one day in London. The story revolves around a highwayman – Macheath – and the women who love him and their respective families.
- Find out more about *The Beggar's Opera*. Which 20th-century play did it influence?

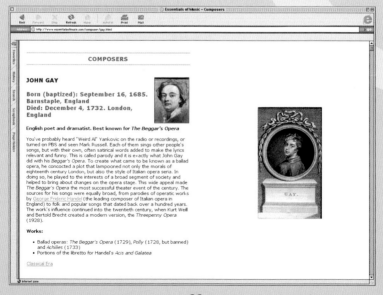

William Hogarth

We have seen how Fielding developed 'comic epic in prose'. We have also seen the many sources of Fielding's writing. One such source was the visual arts. Fielding was strongly influenced by the work of William Hogarth who, like him, rejected the artistic orthodoxy of the time. Hogarth was an engraver, illustrator and painter who concentrated on real figures from English society, and from London street life in particular. His talents were recognised by Fielding and the two worked together on Fielding's *Tragedy ofTragedies* (1731). He also painted scenes from John Gay's *Beggar's Opera*.

- Find out more about Hogarth's life and works.

CHAPTER **FIVE**

On the Road

Sophia's father and aunt, meanwhile, had decided that the marriage with Blifil should take place as soon as possible.

'The lawyers will do all the paperwork,' [1] Mr Western told Blifil. 'You can have her tomorrow, my boy!'

Blifil pretended to be pleased at the news, but he did not really love Sophia at all. She was a beautiful and rich young girl. He intended to punish her for her love of Tom Jones after the wedding.

Mrs Honour told Sophia that the parson had been asked to

---

1. **paperwork** : legal requirements, here documentation.

prepare the wedding banns [1] for the couple. Sophia was horrified at the news.

'I'll run away!' she told her maid. 'Will you be my friend, and come with me?'

'Of course I will,' Mrs Honour replied affectionately, 'but where can we go?'

'We'll go to London,' Sophia told her. 'I know a lady there. She's often asked me to visit her.'

Tom, meanwhile, was walking along the road to Bristol. He did not really know what to do as he had lost the money Mr Allworthy had given him. Then he saw an inn [2] on the road, and he decided to stop there for the night.

Tom was sleeping peacefully at the inn when a noisy group of soldiers arrived at the inn. They were fighting for the king against his enemies in the north. [3] They made so much noise that Tom came down to talk to them. He found them very good company. He decided to join them.

Tom and the soldiers marched off together the next morning. They marched all day, and arrived in the evening at an inn where their captain was waiting for them. The captain welcomed Tom. He understood immediately that Tom was a gentleman. He invited the young man to dine with him and the other officers.

The dinner was a noisy one, and Tom suggested that everyone drink a toast [4] to Sophia Western. One of the officers, a man called Northerton, pretended that he knew her.

1. **wedding banns** : formal announcement of the coming marriage in church.
2. **inn** : small hotel.
3. **king ... north** : reference to the second Jacobite uprising lead by Bonnie Prince Charlie against the English and King George II.
4. **toast** : drink in someone's honour.

Tom Jones

Sophy Western!' he cried. 'That girl had love affairs with nearly all the young men in Bath.'

Tom was furious at the officer's joke about Sophia.

'You're a liar!' he shouted at Northerton.

Northerton picked up a bottle and threw it at Tom's head. Tom fell to the ground.

'Were you telling him the truth about this Sophy Western?' the captain asked Northerton severely.

'Of course not, sir,' Northerton replied. 'It was just a joke.'

'Your joke has killed a man,' the captain said sternly. [1] He pointed at where Tom was lying on the floor. 'You'll hang for it!' [2]

Northerton was suddenly afraid, and he ran away.

The soldiers carried Tom up to bed and summoned [3] a doctor. Everyone thought his life was in great danger from the injury he had received. In the middle of the night, however, he woke up and asked to see the captain.

'I'm going to fight that officer,' Tom announced. He tried to get out of bed.

'You must wait until you're stronger,' the captain advised him. 'Besides, Northerton has escaped. We don't know where he's gone.'

The next day Tom felt much better, and he sent for a barber to shave him. The barber was a cheerful man, and he spoke in rather a strange manner – he used a lot of Latin expressions in his speech. Tom was very surprised.

'You're an educated man!' he said.

---

1. **sternly** : with seriousness.
2. **You'll hang for it!** : you will be killed, executed for your actions. Literally, you will be hung by the neck until dead.
3. **summoned** : called for.

'That's right, sir,' the barber told him. 'I'm an educated man, but I'm a very poor man as well. Education made me poor.'

Tom invited the barber to drink a glass of wine with him, and they had a lively conversation together. Then the barber went downstairs to talk to the landlady [1] of the inn.

'That young man is no gentleman,' the landlady confided in the barber. 'Someone told me that he was dismissed from Mr Allworthy's house.'

'So he's a servant, then?' the barber mused [2] quietly. 'But do you know his name?'

'Tom Jones,' the landlady told him.

'Tom Jones!' the barber repeated in great surprise. 'If his name is really Tom Jones, then he is certainly a gentleman,' he said mysteriously.

The barber was now anxious to become friends with Tom. He soon persuaded the young man to tell him the whole story of his life, and of his unhappy love affair with Sophia Western.

'I know the Western family!' the barber cried delightedly.

Later that day Tom felt a little unwell because of his injury. He sent for the doctor, and was surprised when the barber appeared once more in his room.

'I am not only the barber, I am also the doctor,' the man told him. He proceeded to treat Tom's injury. Then he made a strange announcement.

'My name is Partridge,' he told Tom. 'People said that I was your father, and the rumour [3] destroyed me.'

1. **landlady** : woman who owns an inn or public house.
2. **mused** : wondered, deliberated.
3. **rumour** : story that people repeated.

Tom Jones

'I know the name,' Tom replied quickly. 'Aren't you my real father?'

'No, sir,' Partridge assured him.

Tom was upset at [1] the idea that Partridge had suffered because of him. He agreed to the older man's suggestion that they should stay together. Partridge believed that Tom was really Mr Allworthy's son. He thought Tom was running away from home.

'Mr Allworthy will be very generous to the person who brings him back,' he thought.

END

Tom and Partridge now left the inn and walked to Gloucester. They set out [2] once more from Gloucester in the evening.

They had a strange adventure while they were out walking. They heard a woman screaming, and Tom rushed forward to help her. He attacked the man who was hurting the woman. He was very surprised that the man was the officer Northerton. He managed to rescue the woman, but once again Northerton ran away.

Tom now took the woman, who was still half-naked, to a very respectable inn in the little town of Upton. At first, the landlady did not want to let the woman into her inn. She thought the woman could not be respectable because her clothes were torn and she was dirty. There followed a fight between her and Tom over whether the woman should be allowed into the inn or not. Partridge then arrived and they all continued their argument.

Just then a carriage arrived at the inn, and a young lady and her maid entered. The landlady stopped arguing, and went off to show the young lady and her servant into the best room of the inn.

---

1. **upset at** : disturbed by.   2. **set out** : began to walk.

76

Now a soldier came into the inn. He looked at the woman whom Tom had rescued in astonishment.

'Aren't you Captain Waters's lady?' he asked her.

'I am indeed,' replied the woman. 'And this gentleman has just saved me from a terrible situation.'

The landlady had overheard this conversation, and she now realised that Mrs Waters was a genuine lady.

'I'm so sorry!' she cried to Mrs Waters. 'How could I tell that you were really a lady when you arrived looking like that?'

1 How many new characters are introduced in Chapter Five? Which character from an earlier chapter re-appears?

2 *Tom Jones* contains elements that made it popular with contemporary readers: fights, misunderstandings, heroes and villains. Another popular narrative device was the journey and the adventures that characters have while travelling. All of these are present in Chapter Five 'On the Road'.

a. Fights: Complete the table with the missing information.

Fight number	Involving	Why	Result
1	Tom and Northerton		
2		Don't know	
3			Landlady finally apologised

b. More misunderstandings: complete the three sentences below.
   - The landlady of the first inn thought ....
   ....
   - The landlady of the second inn ....
   ....
   - Partridge thought ....
   ....

c. We have seen that Tom's life is complicated not only by his own actions but by the ill-intentioned interference of others (in earlier chapters by Blifil and Thwackum, for example).
   Which character introduced in Chapter Five deliberately makes life difficult for Tom?

3 **a.** Who are the characters referred to in bold in the four citations below? An example (0) has been done for you.

    0. 'You can have **her** tomorrow my boy!' **her** = Sophia

    1. '**this gentleman** has just saved me from a terrible situation.'

    2. 'your joke killed **a man**'

    3. 'Education made **me** poor.'

    4. 'the man (hurting **the woman**) was Northerton'

b. Explain the four relationships (1-4) shown. (0. Mr Allworthy is talking about his daughter.) Summarise each in a paragraph: which relationships do you think will be important as the story continues? Discuss your ideas with your partner.

4 Tom stays in three inns. Each stay is eventful. Fill in the table with the missing information.

	Inn 1	Inn 2	Inn 3
Who?		Northerton/ Captain	
What happens?			Tom rescues Mrs Waters
Where?	On the road to Bristol		

6 **5** Listen to this extract from Chapter Five and complete the missing information in questions 1-6. An example (0) has been done for you.

FCE

0. Tom was surprised by ....*how Partridge spoke.*..................

1. Partridge wasn't only educated but ....

2. After having a glass of wine with Tom, Partridge ....
....

3. The landlady thought Tom wasn't ....

4. When Partridge discovered Tom's name he wanted ....
....

5. When Partridge told Tom his story, Tom agreed to let ....
....

6. Partridge thought Tom ....

6 Complete the sentences below by choosing a word (A, B, C or D). Look at this example:

0. Blifil felt ......*D*...... love for Sophia.
   A any
   B neither
   C none
   D no

1. When Sophia left her home, Tom was .... walking to Bristol.
   A yet
   B already
   C while
   D been

2. The captain was pleased .... Tom to his regiment.
   A to welcome
   B welcome
   C welcoming
   D having welcomed

3. Northerton threw a bottle because Tom .... him a liar.

   A was calling

   B had been calling

   C had called

   D has called

4. 'If you .... you won't be able to fight Northerton,' the Captain told Tom.

   A don't get better

   B didn't get better

   C won't get better

   D wouldn't get better

5. 'Not .... am I a barber, but a doctor as well' said Partridge.

   A just

   B alone

   C simply

   D only

6. Tom thought Partridge was .... interesting person that he invited him to join him on his travels.

   A such

   B so

   C really

   D such an

7. 'He .... be a servant!' the landlady told Mr Partridge.

   A must

   B can

   C mustn't

   D will

8. The landlady, seeing Mrs Waters' condition, decided not .... her in.

   A let

   B to let

   C letting

   D to letting

9. Mrs Waters didn't give the .... of being a lady.

   A importance

   B appearance

   C impression

   D ideas

10. The landlady realised Mrs Waters was a lady .... the Captain's arrival.

   A because

   B thanks

   C as a result

   D thanks to

Looking ahead

1 Tom asks Mr Partridge, 'Are you my real father?' but Partridge replies 'No, sir'.
The mystery of Tom's real father remains. Have you any ideas?

2 'Just then a carriage at the inn, and a young lady and her maid entered'.
Who do you think they are?

CHAPTER **SIX**

Tom's Adventure
with a Traveller

Mrs Waters was grateful to Tom for saving her from the brutal officer. She also noticed what a good-looking young man he was. She invited him to have dinner with her in her room at the inn.

Tom was so hungry that, at first, he did not notice what Mrs Waters' real intentions were. He ate the food she put before him, and did not think of anything else. When he had finished eating, however, he looked at his host carefully. Now he began to understand why she had invited him into her room.

Tom tried to remember his love for Sophia, but he was a young man, and he was easily tempted. Soon he had forgotten all about

Tom Jones

Sophia, and he went to bed with Mrs Waters.

Although she called herself 'Mrs Waters', the lady was not really married to Captain Waters at all. She had lived with him for a number of years, but she had also had a close relationship with Northerton.

When Northerton ran away because he thought he had killed Tom, he went to Mrs Waters for help. She agreed to help him, but in return for her kindness he had tried to rob [1] her when they were out walking together.

All the guests at the inn had gone to sleep when a man on horseback arrived. He asked the maid if there was a lady staying, saying that he was looking for his wife. The maid assumed that the man was Mrs Waters' husband. She agreed to let him into that lady's bedroom.

The man, whose name was Fitzpatrick, burst noisily into the room where Tom and Mrs Waters were sleeping. Mrs Waters begin to scream when she saw a strange man in the room, and Tom leapt [2] out of bed. The man looked at both of them, and realised he had made a mistake. He apologised and left the lovers alone once more.

It did not occur to Mr Fitzpatrick to search for his wife in any of the other rooms at the inn. Instead, he went to bed himself. He was ashamed of the disturbance he had caused in a respectable inn.

The peace of the inn was disturbed again by the arrival of another two young women, one of whom was wearing very expensive and beautiful clothes. The lady with the beautiful clothes went to bed almost immediately, but her maid went down

1. **rob** : steal money from.　　　2. **leapt** : jumped.

to the kitchen to have something to eat. Here she met Partridge and they began talking.

'You, sir, seem to be a gentleman,' commented the maid politely.

'Indeed I am,' replied Partridge. 'I'm travelling with the son of a gentleman called Allworthy.'

'Allworthy!' cried the maid. 'I know Mr Allworthy, and I can tell you that he hasn't got a son.'

Mr Partridge smiled quietly.

'Not everyone knows this,' he told her, 'but Mr Jones is certainly Mr Allworthy's son.'

'And you say he's here, in this inn!' the maid exclaimed excitedly. Without another word she rushed upstairs to her mistress. The maid was Mrs Honour, and her mistress was Sophia.

Mrs Honour told Sophia that Tom was staying at the inn. Sophia was astonished at the news, and she sent Mrs Honour downstairs again to ask Partridge to go and wake him up.

Again Partridge smiled quietly when Mrs Honour asked him to wake Tom.

'I'm not going upstairs to wake him,' he said. 'Besides, he's already got one woman with him – that's enough for any man at one time.'

At first Sophia could not believe what Mrs Honour told her about Tom. Then she spoke to the maid at the inn and realised that Tom really was with another woman. She cried very bitterly, and then she had an idea – she wanted Tom to suffer when he woke up! She took off her muff [1] and gave it to Mrs Honour.

'Go to his room,' she ordered, 'and leave this muff on the

---

1. **muff** : ornament worn on the arm, used by women to keep their hands warm.

Tom Jones

pillow. He'll see it tomorrow morning when he leaves that other woman's bed. Then he'll know I was here.'

Sophia and Mrs Honour now left the inn. They were travelling on horseback.

Very early in the morning the other young lady who had arrived with her maid in the carriage, left the inn. She did not want to wait for her carriage driver to wake up so she and her maid decided to ride instead.

Tom also woke up, and went to his own room. He saw Sophia's muff lying on the pillow of his bed.

Sophia's father, Mr Western suddenly arrived at the inn. He was looking for his daughter, and he was astonished to see Tom coming down the stairs holding Sophia's muff in his hand.

'Where is she?' he demanded angrily.

'I don't know,' Tom answered. 'This is certainly Sophia's muff, but I haven't seen her at all.'

Mr Fitzpatrick heard Mr Western and Tom talking and he decided to interfere.

'The young man's not telling the truth, sir,' he told Mr Western. 'He's been in bed with her all night. Come with me and I'll show you where she is.'

He led Mr Western to Mrs Waters' room and opened the door. Mr Western looked at Mrs Waters. He realised that he had made a terrible blunder. [1] He apologised and left the room.

Tom and Partridge set off together on foot to continue their journey. Mr Western also rode away from the inn. Mr Fitzpatrick offered Mrs Waters a lift in his carriage to go to Bath. They left the inn together.

---

1. **blunder** : mistake, error.

Chapter Six is full of misunderstandings and characters (new and old)
come and go.

1 **Answer these questions.**

    a. After reading Chapter Six, can we answer the questions in
        Looking ahead, exercise two on page 82.

    b. Who arrives at the inn in Chapter Six? Write their names:
        1. 'a man on horseback': ....
        2. 'another two young women' : ....
        3. 'Sophia's father': ....

    c. Tom gets himself into trouble ... again ('but he was a young man,
        and he was easily tempted.' page 83)
        When was the last time this happened?

    d. What do we know about Mrs Waters?
        Fact: ....
        Opinion: ....

2 **More misunderstandings**
Mrs Waters is the object of two major misunderstandings in Chapter
Six. What are they?
Complete the sentences a. and b. They both end in the same way.

    a. The maid thought the woman staying in the inn was ....
        Actually, she was Mrs Waters.

    b. Mr Fitzpatrick thought the woman staying in the inn was
        ....

3 **'Mind your own business'**

    a. In which situations (a-d) would the expression 'mind your own
        business' as a reply to the two questions below be <u>inappropriate</u>?
        Explain why. Discuss your ideas with your partner.

'How much does your father earn?'   *'mind your own business!'*

1. teacher to student   student to teacher
2. one classmate to another   reply to classmate

'What did you get in your maths   *'mind your own business!'*
test?'

1. Parent to son/daughter   son/daughter's reply
2. one classmate to another   reply to classmate

b. Which characters in Chapter Six do <u>not</u> mind their own business? Who suffers as a result?

4 **Who leaves the inn at the end of Chapter Six? Who travels in company and who travels alone?**

....

....

5 **Read this short text about Sophia Western and decide which answer (A, B, C or D) best fits each space.**
There is an example at the beginning (0).

'Sophia Western is very different (0)........B........ the other characters in *Tom Jones*. Firstly, her moral behaviour (1)................ her from the others. She is (2)................ given to the sexual licence of the man she loves or of the women she (3)................ on her (4)................ . Secondly, she is generous in spirit. She has no interest in gossip or rumour spreading, (5)................ so many of the other (6)................ in the novel. Her reaction to the news of Tom's night with Mrs Waters is dignified (7)................ her moral (8)................ has irritated some critics.'

0.	A in	B from	C at	D for
1.	A separates	B divides	C joins	D unites
2.	A no	B none	C not	D nothing

89

3. **A** meets   **B** walks   **C** talks   **D** goes
4. **A** travel   **B** voyage   **C** expedition   **D** travels
5. **A** similar   **B** unlike   **C** like   **D** dissimilar
6. **A** personalities **B** persons   **C** characters   **D** people
7. **A** although   **B** however   **C** despite   **D** in spite
8. **A** superior   **B** superiority   **C** height   **D** high

Looking ahead

1 **In Chapter Seven we discover the identity of 'the other young lady'. Listen to this extract from the beginning of the chapter and complete the sentences.**

1. The young lady's name was ....
2. She was Sophia's ....
3. Sophia had been good friends with the young lady before she married ....
4. Her husband married her not for love but for ....
5. Her husband treated his wife ....

CHAPTER **SEVEN**

The Travellers Arrive in London

ophia and Mrs Honour travelled away from the inn as fast as they could. Soon they were approached by another lady and her maid who were also travelling fast. When the two parties were close enough to see each other, there were cries of surprise.

'Harriet!' exclaimed Sophia.

'Sophia!' replied the other lady.

The lady was Harriet Fitzpatrick. She was Sophia's cousin. They had been very good friends until she had run away to marry Mr Fitzpatrick.

'He only married me in order to have my money,' Harriet told

Tom Jones

her cousin. 'He treated me very badly. He locked me in a room, and he did not let me write to anyone. I managed to escape and my husband followed me. He nearly discovered me last night at the inn at Upton!'

ᴇ/ᴺᴰ

Now Sophia also told her story. She told her cousin everything about Blifil, but she did not mention the name of Tom Jones.

That evening the travellers arrived at another inn. An Irish lord arrived at the inn very late in the evening. He and Harriet seemed to know each other very well, and she seemed pleased to see him. He offered to take all the ladies to London the following day in his carriage. They willingly accepted his offer.

The next morning Sophia was surprised to find that she had lost her money. She thought it had fallen out of her pocket somewhere on the road. There was nothing she could do about it, so she settled herself into [1] the Irish lord's carriage for the journey to London.

When Sophia and Harriet arrived in London they took lodgings [2] in the city. Sophia wrote a note to Lady Bellaston, a relative of hers whom she did not know very well. Lady Bellaston invited her to stay at her own house.

Harriet seemed pleased that Sophia had found somewhere else to live. This made Sophia wonder about her friendship with the Irish lord. Did Harriet want to be free to meet him in secret? Sophia decided to give her cousin some advice.

'Be very careful, ' she said. 'You're a married woman, my dear, and your Irish friend is also married. Take care of your reputation.'

Harriet laughed gaily. [3]

1. **settled herself into** : made herself comfortable in.
2. **lodgings** : rented accommodation.
3. **gaily** : happily.

'What simple [1] ideas you have!' she said. 'It's obvious that you're used to a quiet country life.'

Tom and Partridge, meanwhile, were also travelling along together. Tom was very depressed because of what had happened at the inn at Upton. He was sure that it was all over with Sophia now. Quite by chance [2] the two men took the same road that Sophia and Harriet had taken earlier. A man stopped them to say that he had found a notebook on the road and he did not know what to do with it. Tom took the notebook, and saw the name 'Sophia Western' written inside it. It also contained a lot of money.

'I'll give it back to her,' he announced excitedly.

They moved on quickly to the inn where Sophia and Harriet had stayed. Here they learned that the two ladies and their maids had continued their journey to London by carriage. Tom immediately decided that he and Partridge should go to London as well.

'I must give her back her property,' he told Partridge.

Tom soon found out where the Irish lord lived, and he soon discovered where the lodgings were that Sophia and Harriet had taken together. When he visited Harriet, however, she refused to give him any news of Sophia's whereabouts. [3] She thought that Tom was Blifil. She decided to visit Lady Bellaston to ask what she should do about this young man who was looking for her cousin so desperately.

Lady Bellaston was interested in Harriet's story, particularly when she heard that Tom was a good-looking young man. Lady Bellaston decided to visit Harriet that evening to see what the

1.   **simple** : naïve.
2.   **Quite by chance** : completely by accident.
3.   **whereabouts** : (here) address where she was staying.

Tom Jones

young man was like.

That evening Tom came again to see Harriet. He showed her Sophia's notebook, and explained that he wanted to give it back to her. He also showed her the money. A little while later a fashionable lady arrived at Harriet's lodgings. Then Harriet's friend, the Irish lord, also arrived. The fashionable lady and the lord talked a lot together.

Tom felt excluded from the brilliant conversation, and he left the lodgings. The fashionable lady left shortly afterwards. The Irish lord advised Harriet not to see Tom again, and then he, too, left the lodgings.

Tom and Partridge found lodgings at a house owned by Mrs Miller, a good woman who had known Mr Allworthy quite well in the past. There was another lodger in the house, a young gentleman called Nightingale. Nightingale invited Tom and Partridge to share a bottle of wine with him.

Suddenly a messenger arrived with a note for Tom. Tom opened it quickly: it contained a mask and an invitation to a party. The note was signed;

From the Queen of the Fairies

Tom was sure that the note came from Sophia. He was very excited at the idea of going to the party!

1 a. Which of the following have so far been 'ingredients' of *Tom Jones*? All these were common themes in the 18th and early 19th-century novel.

- ☐ comic misunderstandings
- ☐ fights
- ☐ tragic events
- ☐ the supernatural (ghosts)
- ☐ sexual promiscuity
- ☐ characters' adventures whilst on a journey
- ☐ illness and disease
- ☐ interfering characters
- ☐ sea voyages
- ☐ military battles
- ☐ social unrest
- ☐ country life
- ☐ religious controversy

Discuss your views with your partner and refer to the story for evidence.

b. Which themes re-appear in Chapter Seven? Give examples.

2 *Sophia also told her story. She told her cousin everything about Blifil, but she did not mention the name of Tom Jones.* What did Sophia actually say to Harriet? Use the cues to complete Sophia's part of the conversation. Then role play the dialogue with your partner. Take turns to play Sophia's part.

Harriet: So that's my story. But what are you doing so far from home? Why aren't you at home in Somerset?

Sophia: (1) be / terrible / misunderstanding / father / want / marry/ man / I / not / love

....

....

Harriet: Who is this man?

Sophia: (2) name / Blifil / Allworthy / nephew / live / nearby

....

....

Harriet: Describe him to me. What is he like?

Sophia: (3) boring / unpleasant / last man / want / marry

....

....

Harriet: But why does your father want you to marry him?

Sophia: (4) my aunt / tell / him / I / love / him / father / think / marriage / Blifil / good idea

....

....

Harriet: Ah dear Sophia! What a father considers good is at times different from the feelings of a daughter. But why did your aunt – an intelligent woman as I remember – make this terrible mistake?

Sophia: (5) I / love /another man / aunt / misunderstand / my feelings

....

....

Harriet: Who is this lucky man you love?

Sophia: I can't tell you. There are many obstacles to our happiness together.

3 **What are the obstacles Sophia refers to?**

4 The travels of our heroes come to an end in London. How did the
last leg of Tom's and Sophia's journeys end?
Answer the questions (1-9).

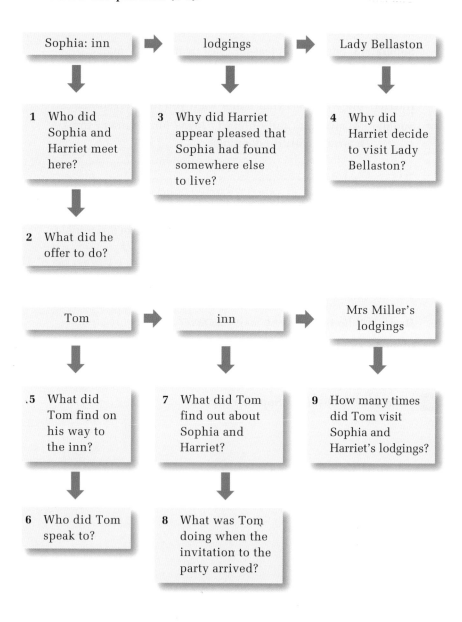

Sophia: inn ➡ lodgings ➡ Lady Bellaston

1 Who did Sophia and Harriet meet here?

3 Why did Harriet appear pleased that Sophia had found somewhere else to live?

4 Why did Harriet decide to visit Lady Bellaston?

2 What did he offer to do?

Tom ➡ inn ➡ Mrs Miller's lodgings

.5 What did Tom find on his way to the inn?

7 What did Tom find out about Sophia and Harriet?

9 How many times did Tom visit Sophia and Harriet's lodgings?

6 Who did Tom speak to?

8 What was Tom doing when the invitation to the party arrived?

FCE 5 Choose from the characters in Chapter Seven listed below (A-F) to answer the questions 1-8. An example (0) has been done for you. You can use an answer more than once.

A   Sophia

B   Harriet

C   Lady Bellaston

D   Tom

E   Nightingale

F   Mrs Miller

Which character/s

0.   [A] did not tell his/her full story?

1.   ☐ lost money?

2.   ☐ received advice on morality?

3.   ☐ wanted to return something that was not his/hers?

4.   ☐ refused to give information about a person's whereabouts?

5.   ☐ was interested in meeting a good looking young man?

6.   ☐ had a reputation for being a good person?

7.   ☐ invited Tom and Partridge for a drink?

8.   ☐ was invited to a party?

Looking ahead

1 **Who do you think the 'Queen of the Fairies' is?**

2 **What do you think will happen to Tom at the party? Choose from among the following:**

a.   He will meet Sophia and they will spend some time together.

b.   He will meet Mrs Fitzpatrick and fall in love with her.

c.   He will meet a mystery woman and he will become her lover.

d.   He will meet Blifil and Mr Allworthy, who will persuade him to return home.

e.   Other. Write down your ideas and check after reading the next chapter.

....

....

....

....

....

....

....

CHAPTER **EIGHT**

City Lovers

T om was very excited when he arrived at the party. He wanted to see Sophia. He was sure she was there. It was difficult to identify people, however, as everybody was wearing a mask. Tom approached several women and spoke to them.

Then a masked woman came up to him.

'Follow me,' she ordered.

Tom knew that the woman was not Sophia, but he thought she must be a friend of Sophia's. He followed her happily.

The two of them talked together for a while, and then the lady left the party. She went home in a carriage, and Tom followed her on foot. At last they arrived at a house, and the front door opened. The masked lady entered and Tom followed her.

'I know who you are,' Tom said, 'you're Mrs Fitzpatrick. Please take off your mask.'

The lady now removed her mask. Tom was surprised. It was not Mrs Fitzpatrick at all, but Lady Bellaston!

Tom and Lady Bellaston talked again, but this time their conversation was more intimate and exciting. In the end, Tom stayed the whole night with Lady Bellaston. She promised to look for Sophia, and they agreed to meet the following evening. Lady Bellaston also gave Tom some money.

When Tom arrived back at Mrs Miller's house he saw that the good woman was very upset. Her cousin's family had no money at all, and she did not know what to do to help them. Tom immediately offered her the money that he had received from Lady Bellaston.

'I've already met one good man in my life,' Mrs Miller told him. 'That was Mr Allworthy. Now I've met another – that's you!'

Tom and Lady Bellaston met again that evening, and things went just as before. They talked for a long while, and then they spent the night together. Once again Lady Bellaston gave him money and clothes. Tom was embarrassed because he was not in love with her. He still loved Sophia.

The next afternoon Lady Bellaston sent Tom a message to say that they could no longer meet in her friend's house. She told him to come to her own house.

Tom arrived at the house before Lady Bellaston did. He entered and was waiting for her, when someone else came in. He was amazed to see that it was Sophia! Lady Bellaston knew that Sophia had gone to the theatre. She had thought the house was empty that evening. Sophia, however, had not enjoyed the play and had come home early.

Tom Jones

Tom and Sophia were very pleased to see each other. Tom gave her the notebook and money that he had found. Then he apologised for what had happened between himself and Mrs Waters at the Upton inn. They had just made peace when the front door of the house opened.

Lady Bellaston entered. She pretended [1] not to know who Tom was.

'This gentleman has just brought me a notebook that I lost,' Sophia said. She, too, was pretending not to know who Tom was.

Tom saw the difficulties of the situation and he left the ladies alone.

'I thought for a moment that that young man was Tom Jones,' Lady Bellaston said to Sophia.

Sophia blushed.

'I can see that you're still thinking about Tom Jones, my dear,' Lady Bellaston told her.

'Tom Jones!' Sophia exclaimed. ' Mr Jones is as unimportant to me as that young man who was just here!'

Tom now found himself involved in another difficult situation at Mrs Miller's house. She told him that her daughter Nancy had been in love with Nightingale. The girl was now expecting a baby, and Nightingale had left her. His father wanted him to marry a rich girl. He felt it was his duty to do what his father ordered. Tom went to see Nightingale. He found the young man very unhappy, but determined to obey his father. Tom persuaded Nightingale to think again. He reminded him that Nancy loved him very much. At last Nightingale reconsidered the question. He

---

1. **pretended** : claimed.

decided to marry Nancy after all. Mrs Miller was very grateful to Tom for his kindness to her daughter.

4   There was a friend of Lady Bellaston's who had been in love with Sophia. His name was Lord Fellamar.

'You'll have problems with her,' Lady Bellaston warned him. 'You've got a rival, you see. His name's Tom Jones.'

'What can I do?' Lord Fellamar asked.

'Be brave,' Lady Bellaston advised him.

Sophia had been alone in her room one evening when Lord Fellamar came in. He made a lot of noise. He told her that he loved her and that he wanted to marry her.

Sophia was frightened by his behaviour.

'If you don't go away, I'll scream,' she told him.

Lord Fellamar did not go away. He grabbed hold of [1] Sophia and began kissing her. Then he put his hands all over her.

Sophia screamed.

Suddenly there was a huge noise downstairs. Mr Western had arrived and he recognised Sophia's voice. He came running up the stairs to her room, and burst in. There was terrible embarrassment and confusion in the room for a while, and then Mr Western took Sophia away with him. He did not let Mrs Honour come with them.

'I don't want you escaping again,' he told his daughter.

Mrs Honour went to Tom's lodgings and told him what had happened. Once again Tom had lost Sophia!

Mr Western had discovered where Sophia was because Harriet Fitzpatrick had written to Mrs Western giving her the

1. **grabbed hold of** : took forcefully.

information. Mrs Western had immediately told her brother that Sophia was staying with Lady Bellaston, and he had hurried to London to find her.

5   Tom, meanwhile, wanted to end the relationship with Lady Bellaston. She wrote to him constantly, and she always wanted to be with him. He did not love her.

'What should I do?' he asked his friend Nightingale.

'Lady Bellaston has had many lovers,' Nightingale told him. 'There's only one honourable way to end the relationship. You must write to her and propose marriage. She'll refuse you, and then you're free!'

Tom took his friend's advice. He wrote to her immediately. A few hours later he received an angry reply from Lady Bellaston.

'You want to marry me because I'm rich. You just want my money. Never come to my house again!'

ACTIVITIES

1 Did you guess who the 'Queen of the Fairies' was?

2 Chapter Eight is entitled 'City Lovers'. Who are they?

3 A lot happens in Chapter Eight! We can divide it into 5 parts look back at the text for the division. Put the events listed below (A-J) into their correct order. There is one event you will not need.

Part	Event
1	1 .... 2 .... 3 ....
2	4 ....
3	5 ....
4	6 .... 7 ....
5	8 .... 9 ....

Events

A   Tom convinces Nightingale to marry Nancy Miller.

B   Lord Fellamar assaults Sophia.

C   Tom meets Lady Bellaston at the party.

D   Mr Western takes his daughter back to Somerset.

E   Mr Western locks his daughter in her room.

F Tom spends a second night with Lady Bellaston.

G Following Nightingale's advice, Tom writes to Lady Bellaston asking her to marry him.

H Tom gives Mrs Miller money.

I Tom meets Sophia at Lady Bellaston's house and returns her notebook and money.

J Lady Bellaston ends her relationship with Tom.

FCE 4 **Choose from the list below (A-F) the suitable headings for parts 1-5. There is one heading you will not need. Compare your answers with your partner. How did you make your choice?**

A ☐ A violent rival

B ☐ The two sides to Tom's personality

C ☐ Father decides!

D ☐ Pretending not to know each other

E ☐ A happy rejection

F ☐ Nightingale reconsiders his decision

5 a. **Tom's weaknesses and strengths are again illustrated in this chapter. What examples are there of both? Fill in the table below. An example has been done for you.**

Weaknesses	Strengths
• Tom innocently expects to meet Sophia at the party	•
•	•
•	•

b. **Summarise the information in a short paragraph. Useful language: *although*; *however*; *while*.**

6 Why do you think Tom mistook Lady Bellaston for Harriet Fitzpatrick at the party?

7 We have seen how Tom gets into some difficult situations because of his own actions and the interference of others. In Chapter Eight, Sophia is affected by somebody's interference. Who does not 'mind their own business' and how does Sophia suffer as a result?

INTERFERENCE ⟶ RESULT

8 a. Nightingale's suggestion to write to Lady Bellaston had the desired effect. What problems, however, do you think the letter could create if read by others? Discuss your ideas with your partner.

b. Tom's problems get worse in the next chapter, 'Tom Goes to Prison'. Why do you think this happens? Which of the following reasons do you think are probable or improbable?

- Tom steals money
- Tom kills a man
- Tom kidnaps Sophia
- Tom deserts from the army
- A past lover says that Tom is the father of her child

Tom Jones As Hero

In the preface to *Tom Jones* Fielding argues that the reader will find nothing in it that is 'prejudicial to the cause of religion and virtue, nothing inconsistent with the strictest rules of decency, nor which can offend even the chastest [1] eye'. This was not a view of the book that Fielding's contemporaries shared. Samuel Johnson, for example, described the novel as 'vicious', and Victorian critics were appalled by its relaxed attitude to physical love.

Contemporary critics have generally agreed that Fielding's morality is concerned with generosity of feeling instead of obedience to specific rules – and this is particularly the case where sexual behaviour is concerned.

The novel introduces a new kind of hero into English literature with the character of Tom Jones. He is good-looking, courageous, and full of the best intentions – so far a conventional hero. But he is also an ordinary human being who fails his own values sometimes. 'Though he did not always act rightly, yet he never did otherwise without feeling and suffering for it'.

The positive side of his heroism can be seen when he resists showing his love for Sophia, knowing that her father wants her to marry Master Blifil. This positive heroism is also based on Tom's emotional nature, his desire not to do harm to anyone. It can also be seen in the way that he offers to help Mrs Miller and her daughter Nancy when Nightingale abandons her. Tom persuades Nightingale

---

1. **chastest** : most sexually pure.

One of Tom Jones adventures from an 18th-century edition by Stotharal.

to do what is emotionally correct rather than what society would think of as morally correct. In the same way, he forgives Blifil at the end of the novel, through his wish not to hurt people.

The negative side of his heroism can be seen in his affair with Molly Seagrim. Unknown to him, Molly has already had several lovers, and seduces him in the hope of making him provide for herself and her child. Even when he discovers the truth about Molly's deceitful [1] past, he is still weak enough to continue the relationship. 'Here ensued [2] a parley, [3] which, as I do not think myself obliged to relate it, I shall omit. It is sufficient that it lasted a full quarter of an hour, at the conclusion of which they retired into the thickest part of the grove.' [4]

The 18th century was a period of great change in society as well as

1. **deceitful** : dishonest.
2. **ensued** : followed.
3. **parley** : conversation.
4. **grove** : small wood or group of trees.

in literature. The traditional dominance of the aristocracy was coming to an end, and the newly powerful middle classes were looking for their own social and moral values. *Tom Jones* reflects these currents of change. Tom is, on the one hand, a gentleman who remains true to the gentlemanly code of behaviour, as when he tries to protect Molly Seagrim's father from Mr Allworthy's anger. He is also, on the other hand, the proponent of a new morality – the morality of genuine feeling. The two codes of behaviour sometimes clash, [1] as when he advises Nightingale to ignore social convention and marry Nancy.

1 **Decide whether the following statements are true or false. Correct those that are false.**

		T	F
a.	Victorian readers in particular approved of Fielding's treatment of sexual manners.	☐	☐
b.	Fielding's morality was based on generosity of feelings.	☐	☐
c.	Tom Jones was a fully conventional hero.	☐	☐
d.	There were two sides to Tom Jones as hero.	☐	☐
e.	Tom's positive heroism is highlighted by his strict observance of social conventions.	☐	☐
f.	Tom's sexual promiscuity is another aspect of his positive heroism.	☐	☐
g.	*Tom Jones* mirrors changes in mid 18th-century society.	☐	☐
h.	There is generally no conflict between social codes and emotional feelings in *Tom Jones*.	☐	☐

1. **clash** : are in conflict.

Looking ahead

1 Listen to this extract from the beginning of the chapter and answer
the following questions (1-4) by choosing the appropriate phrase or
sentence (a, b, c).

1. Why was Sophia in her room?
   - a. ☐ she wanted to avoid her father
   - b. ☐ she had been told to stay there by her father
   - c. ☐ she was frightened of Lord Fellamar

2. How many different objects were inside the chicken that Black
   George brought Sophia?
   - a. ☐ two
   - b. ☐ three
   - c. ☐ four

3. Why was Mrs Western angry with her brother?
   - a. ☐ he was being cruel to Sophia
   - b. ☐ he was rude to Blifil
   - c. ☐ he didn't give his daughter enough to eat

4. Where did Blifil visit Sophia?
   - a. ☐ at her father's house
   - b. ☐ at her cousin's house
   - c. ☐ at her aunt's house

CHAPTER NINE

Tom Goes to Prison

M r Western was furious with Sophia when she continued to refuse the marriage with Mr Blifil. He locked her in her room.

'You will marry him – even if you hang yourself the very next day!' he threatened her.

One of the servants that Mr Western had brought to London was Black George. He brought Sophia her meals, although she ate very little. He brought Sophia one of her favourite meals – roast chicken with eggs inside.

Sophia was tempted by the sight of her favourite dish, and began to eat. The chicken contained eggs, which she expected. It also contained a letter from Tom – which she had not expected.

Mr Western and his sister now had a furious argument.

114

'You can't keep Sophia locked up here,' Mrs Western told him. 'How many times have I got to tell you this is a free country!'

At last Mr Western agreed that his sister could take Sophia to her own house.

Mrs Western wanted to find out from her cousin Lady Bellaston about the lord who wanted to marry Sophia. When Blifil came to visit Sophia at her house, Mrs Western was quite cool [1] towards him and sent him away.

Mrs Western now set off to visit her cousin.

Lady Bellaston hated Sophia because she knew that Tom loved her. She decided to take her revenge on the young couple.

'Look at this,' Lady Bellaston said, showing Mrs Western a letter. It was Tom's proposal of marriage. 'You can keep it if you like,' Lady Bellaston offered.

END

Later that day Lord Fellamar came to see Lady Bellaston. He was still keen [2] to marry Sophia. Lady Bellaston told him the real difficulty was not Mr Western. It was the man that Sophia loved, Tom Jones.

'Can't you use your influence in some way?' she asked him. 'Can't you have him kidnapped [3] or press-ganged? [4] I can let you know where he lives if you like.'

Mrs Fitzpatrick now sent an invitation to Tom, whom she found an interesting young man. Unfortunately, she had also written to Mrs Western telling her where Sophia was – and Mrs Western had given her address to Mr Fitzpatrick.

1. **cool** : reserved, not very friendly.
2. **keen** : enthusiastic.
3. **kidnapped** : taken away by force, typically for a ransom.
4. **press-ganged** : taken away by force to join the army or navy.

Tom Jones

When Tom arrived at Mrs Fitzpatrick's house he was seen by the suspicious Mr Fitzpatrick. The jealous husband struck [1] Tom and drew [2] his sword. Tom reacted swiftly and without thinking drew his own sword and ran the poor man through. [3]

'I'm dying!' Mr Fitzpatrick cried out.

Lord Fellamar had hired [4] a group of men to follow Tom. They had orders to grab hold of him so that he could be press-ganged. These men now ran forward and held him.

'He'll never go to sea if that man dies,' one of them joked.

They carried him off to prison.

Tom was sitting in his prison cell the next day when Partridge came to see him. He told Tom that Mr Fitzpatrick had died of his wound. He also gave Tom a letter from Sophia. Tom opened it and read:

'I've just seen a letter that you sent to Lady Bellaston and I never want to see you again.'

Mr Allworthy was at Mrs Miller's house talking to her. Mrs Miller was trying to persuade Mr Allworthy that Tom was a good young man.

'You don't know him as well as I do,' Mr Allworthy told her.

'I know that he's got enemies,' Mrs Miller replied, 'and I know they tell lies about him.'

Blifil now rushed into the room in a very excited state, to report the news that Tom had been arrested for murder. Mr Western also arrived.

---

1. **struck** : hit.
2. **drew** : took out.
3. **ran the poor man through** : cut him deeply with his sword.
4. **hired** : paid.

'We've all been frightened of a young bastard,' he shouted, 'and now there's some lord as well – he might be a bastard as well, for all I know!'

At first Mr Allworthy did not understand what Mr Western was talking about. Then he saw that Mr Western was furious about Lord Fellamar's offer of marriage to Sophia. Mr Allworthy said that Sophia should be free to marry the person she wanted.

'She'll marry Blifil!' shouted Mr Western. 'She's my daughter, and she'll do as I tell her.'

Blifil now told Mr Western the news about Tom's arrest.

'Murder!' cried Mr Western. 'Arrested for murder, eh? That's the best news I've ever heard.'

FCE **1** Choose the answer (A, B, C or D) which fits best according to the text. There is an example (0) at the beginning.

0. Why did Mr Western lock Sofia in her room?

   A ✔ he didn't want her to run away again

   B ☐ he wanted to punish her for having run away

   C ☐ he wanted to protect her from Blifil

   D ☐ he wanted to protect her from Lord Fellamar

1. Mr Western eventually let Sophia leave her room because

   A ☐ he felt sorry for her

   B ☐ he was convinced to do so by his sister

   C ☐ Mr Allworthy told him his actions were against the law

   D ☐ he knew she would escape anyway

2. Who did Lady Bellaston show Tom's letter to?

   A ☐ a friend

   B ☐ a rival in love

   C ☐ a lover

   D ☐ a relative

3. Why did Lady Bellaston help Lord Fellamar?

   A ☐ she thought he would make a good husband for Sophia

   B ☐ it had been Mrs Western's idea

   C ☐ she wanted to punish Tom

   D ☐ she wanted to punish Mrs Fitzpatrick

4. Mr Fitzpatrick discovered where his wife was living. Who was responsible for his finding out?

   A ☐ his wife

   B ☐ Mrs Western

   C ☐ Lord Fellamar

   D ☐ Lady Bellaston

119

5. What was Mr Fitzpatrick doing when he saw Tom outside Mrs
    Fitzpatrick's house?

    A ☐ he was speaking to his wife

    B ☐ he was waiting to attack Tom

    C ☐ he was waiting to attack his wife

    D ☐ we don't know

6. Tom was taken to prison because

    A ☐ he had injured Fitzpatrick

    B ☐ he had murdered Fitzpatrick

    C ☐ he had tried to escape a press-gang

    D ☐ he had attacked the men hired by Lord Fellamar

7. How many pieces of bad news did Partridge bring Tom in prison?

    A ☐ one

    B ☐ two

    C ☐ three

    D ☐ four

2 **Who defends Tom in Chapter Nine?**

....

....

....

....

....

3 Will

- *'You will marry him...'*
- *'She'll marry Blifil...'*

Western **insists** on his daughter's marriage to Blifil. 'Will' has several uses: 'insisting' is one of them. Match the use (1-5) to the example (a-e). Add some more examples of your own to each use.

Use	Example
1 Insisting	**a** 'It's getting late. I'll stay here tonight.'
2 Promising	**b** 'You will apologise immediately for what you have done!
3 Predicting	**c** 'Will you follow me, please?'
4 Deciding suddenly	**d** 'The story will have a happy ending.'
5 Making a request	**e** 'I will love you forever.'

T: GRADE 7

4 Topic – Environment

a. Using your dictionary, prepare a list of common crimes and criminals in the table below.

Crime	Criminal
murder	murderer

b. What typical sentences are given for these crimes in your country? Are they right, or too severe, or not severe enough? What types of crime are common where you live? What do you think can be done? Why do some people turn to crime?

5 *'Tom was sitting in his prison cell...'* Imagine you are Tom. You have been accused of murder and Sophia has written to you telling you: *'I never want to see you again.'* Working with a partner imagine:

- What the cell is like (Dark? Old? Furniture? View from window? Prison guards? Food?).
- Your feelings (desperation, sadness, regret, frustration).

Write a short entry in your prison diary for today.

Looking ahead

1 *Tom Jones* is a comic novel and so the reader expects a happy ending. What do you think this happy ending will be? Look at the title of Chapter Ten!
The path from Tom's situation at the end of Chapter Nine to his marriage to Sophia at the end of the story is full of problems.

a. What problems have to be solved? Working in a small group consider the problems. Think of a character, and then of some problems to be solved.
   For example:

Mr Fitzpatrick	Is he dead? Will Tom be accused of his murder? How can Tom avoid jail?
Mr Western	
Blifil	
Mr Allworthy	

b. What question has remained unanswered since the very beginning of the story and needs to be answered if Tom and Sophia are to be together?

CHAPTER **TEN**

Mr Western Commands another Marriage

Tom's friends came to the prison to try to cheer him up. Mr Partridge told him that Mr Fitzpatrick was still alive. Nightingale and Mrs Miller also visited Tom. They did their best to make him more cheerful.

'They can't hang you,' Nightingale said, 'because he attacked you first – the whole thing was a ghastly [1] accident.'

'I know he did,' Tom said, 'but the idea that I have killed a man is terrible to me. And there's another thing that makes me unhappy,' he said sadly. He was thinking about Sophia.

---

1. **ghastly** : terrible.

123

Tom Jones

Tom asked Mrs Miller to carry a letter to Sophia, which she agreed to do.

Sophia's aunt was still trying to persuade Sophia to marry Lord Fellamar. It was no good trying to convince Sophia, however.

'He behaved horribly to me,' she told her aunt. 'He behaved very violently,' she confessed. 'He threw me down and kissed me, and then he tried to take my clothes off.'

Sophia's aunt was shocked by this news.

'What an insult!' she cried.

Mrs Western's enthusiasm for the marriage between Lord Fellamar and Sophia seemed to cool as a result of what Sophia had told her. The girl hoped that she could persuade her aunt to give up the idea.

Sophia's optimism did not last, however, because Sophia's maid saw Tom's letter. She told Mrs Western about it. Mrs Western was now furious with Sophia.

'You've had a letter from a murderer!' she said angrily. 'I'm going to send you straight back to your father in the morning.'

Sophia was now unhappy again, and there was also bad news for Tom when Nightingale visited him next.

'The men who saw you fighting Mr Fitzpatrick are going to tell the judge that you started the fight,' Nightingale told him.

'But why?' demanded Tom. 'Why do they want to lie about what happened?'

Mrs Miller then came into the cell, to report that she had delivered Tom's letter to Sophia. When she came back to the house to take Sophia's reply to Tom, she learned that Sophia had gone away.

Tom was in despair now. He said that he was prepared to die, and that he hoped for the truth to come out after his death.

Nightingale and Mrs Miller's visit to Tom was interrupted by the guard who brought a message. A lady had arrived at the prison who wanted to see Tom. Nightingale and Mrs Miller hurriedly left the cell.

Tom was very surprised to see that the lady was Mrs Waters.

Mrs Waters was in London for a special reason. She had left the inn at Upton with Mr Fitzpatrick. Mr Fitzpatrick's wife had run away from him, and he had asked Mrs Waters to marry him. She accepted his offer. She did not know that he already had a wife.

'I've got some good news for you,' Mrs Waters now said to Tom. 'The man you fought with is not dying – and he's ready to tell the whole truth about the fight, and how he started it.'

Tom was now quite cheerful again, and he and Mrs Waters spent a long time talking about everything that had happened at Upton. Finally Mrs Waters left the cell.

Partridge now hurried in. He looked very anxious and worried.

'Was that the woman you slept with at Upton?' he asked in horror. 'Her real name is Jenny Jones – she's your mother!'

Tom was now plunged [1] into despair once more. He thought he had done a terrible thing, and he was very ashamed. [2] Then a letter from Mrs Waters was delivered to the prison. Mrs Waters said in her letter that she had just learned who Tom was. She wanted to talk to him again because she had something very important to tell him.

1. **plunged** : thrown.
2. **ashamed** : felt guilty.

Tom Jones

Various people now came to see Mr Allworthy. The first of them was Partridge.

'I don't understand you,' Mr Allworthy told him. 'Why are you your own son's servant?'

'I'm neither his servant nor his father, sir,' Partridge explained. 'And I wish his mother was someone else!'

Partridge now told Mr Allworthy everything that had happened at the inn. Mr Allworthy was appalled [1] at the story.

Mrs Waters now came into the room.

'There she is!' cried Partridge excitedly. 'That's Jenny Jones, sir. She'll tell you that I'm not Tom's father!'

'Partridge is telling the truth, sir,' Mrs Waters admitted to Mr Allworthy. 'I promised to tell you one day who the boy's real father was. That's why I'm here now.'

Partridge now left the room, and Mrs Waters began her story.

'Do you remember the young student who stayed at your house many years ago? His name was Summers.'

'I remember him,' said Mr Allworthy.

'He's Tom's father,' Mrs Waters explained, 'but I am not Tom's mother. I put the baby into your bed, sir, but I am not his mother. He was your sister's child.'

Mrs Waters then told Mr Allworthy how Bridget and Summers had had a love affair. The young man had then died, and Bridget had asked Jenny Jones to help her dispose of [2] the baby.

'Why didn't she say something?' asked Mr Allworthy. 'Why did she die without a word about it to anyone?'

'I'm sure she left a message with someone, sir,' Mrs Waters

---

1. **appalled** : disgusted.
2. **dispose of** : free herself from.

told him. 'She always said she wanted to.'

'I'll get in touch with [1] her lawyer, perhaps he can tell me something,' Mr Allworthy decided.

Mr Allworthy immediately sent for Mr Dowling the lawyer. Mrs Waters was very surprised when she saw Mr Dowling come into the room.

'Did you know that Tom Jones is my nephew?' Mr Allworthy asked the lawyer.

'Of course I did, sir,' Mr Dowling replied.

'Why didn't you ever say anything to me?' Mr Allworthy demanded.

---

1. **get in touch with** : contact.

Tom Jones

'I thought you'd read the letter that your sister gave me. I gave it to Mr Blifil when you were ill.'

Mrs Waters interrupted the two men.

There's something I don't understand, sir,' she said to Mr Allworthy.

'Mr Dowling knows that Tom is your nephew – but he offered Mr Fitzpatrick money to tell the judge that Tom Jones started the fight!'

'I was acting on Mr Blifil's instructions,' the lawyer said. 'He wanted me to bribe [1] Mr Fitzpatrick and the men who saw the fight.'

Mr Allworthy was very surprised at this news. He sent for Blifil at once.

'And tell him to bring the letter that my sister wrote when she was dying,' he ordered. 'I'm going out now, but I shall be back soon.'

Mr Allworthy hurried to Mr Western's house to speak to Sophia.

'I think my family has made you very unhappy,' he began. 'It was my fault. I did not know what Mr Blifil was really like – I do now, and I think you should be released from the marriage.'

Sophia looked delighted at Mr Allworthy's words.

'I have something else to say,' Mr Allworthy went on. 'I'm going to give all my money to another young relative of mine,' he told her. 'Will you allow that young man to visit you?'

'I don't want to talk about marriage offers any more,' Sophia informed him. 'I'm going to return to the country soon.'

---

1. **bribe** : make someone do something dishonest for money.

'My young relative's unhappiness will go on,' Mr Allworthy told her.

'How can he be unhappy about me if he does not know me?' Sophia asked.

'But he does know you, Miss Western,' Mr Allworthy told her. 'I'm talking about my sister's son, my nephew Tom Jones.'

Sophia was astonished at what Mr Allworthy had told her.

Just then Mr Western burst angrily into the room.

'Look here, Allworthy,' he said, 'my cousin Lady Bellaston has just written to me. She says that that murderer Tom Jones is out of prison. She says I should lock up my daughter again.'

'I'm going to see Mr Jones now, and I suggest you come and see him later,' Mr Allworthy replied quietly.

The meeting between Tom Jones and Mr Allworthy was a very emotional one. Mr Allworthy apologised for all of his suspicions about Tom. He decided to give Tom all of his money when he died.

'You're very good, uncle,' Tom told him, 'but I'm still very unhappy. I'll never be able to have the girl I love.'

Mr Western now came in. He had heard everything from Sophia, and he could not wait to see Tom.

'I'm so glad to see you!' he cried. 'We must forgive each other. Come and see Sophia now.'

Tom also saw Blifil. He forgave him for all the trouble he had caused.

Everyone now went back to Mr Western's house where they had tea together. At last Tom and Sophia were alone together.

They sat in silence for a while.

'Can you ever forgive me?' Tom asked. Then he told her the truth about his letter to Lady Bellaston. He explained that the

Tom Jones

idea was Nightingale's. Sophia believed Tom's explanation and she forgave him.

'Can you ever be faithful to me?' she asked him.

Tom took her to the mirror and showed her face there.

'Look,' he said to her. 'I can be faithful to all this beauty.'

'Perhaps, then,' Sophia suggested, 'we can talk about marriage.'

Mr Western rushed into the room.

'Well!' he cried. 'Have you fixed it up? Are you getting married tomorrow?'

'Not tomorrow, father,' Sophia said.

'Tomorrow, I say,' her father insisted. 'Or are you going to disobey me?'

'No, father, I shan't disobey you.'

Tom Jones

Tom and Sophia had a very quiet wedding. Mr Western and Mr Allworthy were there, and so was Mrs Miller.

*

Blifil and Mr Allworthy did not see each other again. Mr Allworthy paid him some money, and Tom secretly added some of his own. Blifil went to live in the north of the country, where he wanted to enter politics.

Mrs Western made friends with Sophia again, and visited her and Tom. Lady Bellaston also visited Sophia. She pretended not to know Tom, and she congratulated him on his marriage.

Nightingale's father bought him some land near Tom's estate. He went to live there with Nancy and Mrs Miller. His family and Tom's family stayed good friends.

Mrs Fitzpatrick lived apart from her husband. She stayed friends with the wife of the Irish lord.

Squire Western gave his land to Tom and Sophia, and went to live in another part of the country. He visited Tom and Sophia often.

Mrs Waters received a small pension from Mr Allworthy. She married the parson.

Tom gave Partridge some money to begin a new school. He decided to marry Molly Seagrim.

1 The closing chapter is full of surprises but ends happily as contemporary readers wanted. The path from Tom's situation in the prison cell at the end of Chapter Nine to his 'quiet wedding' with Sophia at the end of the story is full of ups and downs.

Read pages 123-132 again and complete Sophia's and Tom's ups and downs. Some examples have been done for you.

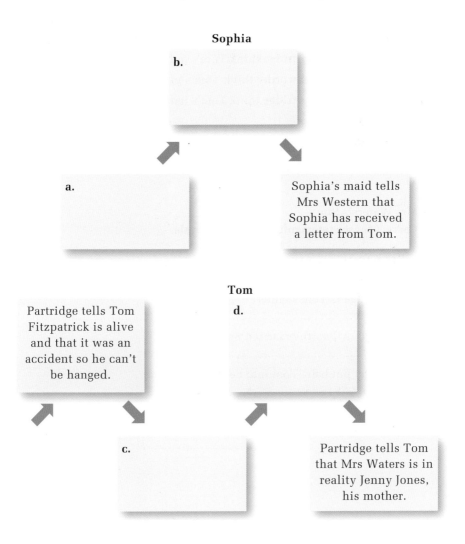

Sophia

b.

a.

Sophia's maid tells Mrs Western that Sophia has received a letter from Tom.

Tom

Partridge tells Tom Fitzpatrick is alive and that it was an accident so he can't be hanged.

d.

c.

Partridge tells Tom that Mrs Waters is in reality Jenny Jones, his mother.

2 Mrs Waters is Jenny Jones. Tom's fear of having committed incest represents Tom's lowest point. Mrs Waters' story is however the turning point. Why did she come to London?

3 a. *'Why are you your own son's servant?'* Allworthy asks *Partridge* (page 123-4). At the stage in the story:

    1. Who does Allworthy think Tom's father is?

    2. Who does Partridge think Tom's father is?

    3. Who does Allworthy think Tom's mother is?

    4. Who does Partridge think Tom's mother is?

    b. Mrs Waters is Jenny Jones. This is bad news for Tom but good news for Partridge. Why?

4 Mrs Waters's Story
Correct these statements as in the example.

    a. Mrs Waters is Tom's mother.
       No, she isn't. Bridget Allworthy is. ....

    b. Partridge is Tom's father.
       ....

    c. Bridget Allworthy married Summers.
       ....

    d. Bridget put baby Tom into her brother's bed.
       ....

    e. Bridget told nobody except Jenny Jones about what had happened.
       ....

5 **a.** *'I'm sure she (Bridget) left a message with someone...', (Mrs Waters said)* (page 126)
Bridget Allworthy had left the message with Mr Dowling, the Allworthy family lawyer. Why didn't it reach Mr Allworthy?

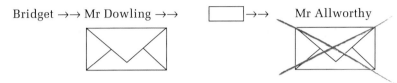

Bridget →→ Mr Dowling →→   [   ] →→   Mr Allworthy

b. Why did Mr Dowling *'...(offer) Mr Fitzpatrick money to tell the judge that Tom Jones started the fight'*? (page 128)

c. What do your answers for questions a. and b. have in common?

6 A Final Misunderstanding
Sophia misunderstands Mr Allworthy when he comes to visit her pages 128-9). How?

7 'The happy ending in *Tom Jones* depends not only on the revealing of truth but also on forgiveness.'
Who do the following characters forgive at the end of the story?

a. Mr Western:

b. Sophia:

c. Tom:

Whose forgiveness is most admirable?

FCE **8** Answer questions 1-6 by using the name of a character (A-I). You can use a character more than once. Some questions require the names of more than one character. An example has been done for you (0).

A   Tom

B   Allworthy

C   Nightingale

D   Mrs Fitzpatrick

E   Mrs Western

F   Squire Western

G   Blifil

H   Partridge

I   Mrs Waters

Who

0.   [A/B] gave money to Blifil?

1.   [ ] left the area?

2.   [ ] did not return to her husband?

3.   [ ] visited Tom and Sophia regularly?

4.   [ ] lived near Tom and Sophia?

5.   [ ] did Mr Allworthy help outside his family?

6.   [ ] returned to a previous occupation?

9 What is amusing about the persons Mrs Waters and Partridge marry?

FILMOGRAPHY

Tom Jones (1963,GB), directed by Tony Richardson, starring Albert Finney, Susannah York.

1 a. *Tom Jones* is not only Tom's story. Which of the following events (A-J) from the story are important for the characters listed below? You can use an event for more than one character. Which events did not you not use?

Mr Allworthy	Sophia	Partridge

Squire Western	Jenny Jones/ Mrs Waters	Mrs Western

A Mr Allworthy finds a baby on his bed.

B Partridge is accused of being the baby's father and is forced to leave the neighbourhood.

C Bridget Allworthy marries Captain Blifil, and their son, Master Blifil, is born.

D Tom has a relationship with Molly Seagrim.

E Allworthy, thinking he is going to die, reads his will.

F Mrs Western is told by her maid that Sophia has received a letter from Tom.

G Mrs Waters is attacked by Northerton.

H Partridge treats Tom for the wound he received from Northerton.

I On her way to London, Sophia meets her cousin Harriet.

J Mrs Western tells her brother Squire Western that Sophia is in love with Blifil.

b. Choose one of the characters. What is his/her story? Write a list of key events in the character's story including the ones you identified in 1a.

c. Using the list of events in 1. write a short composition describing the character's story for someone who has not read the book.

Synopsis

Tom Jones, The History of a Foundling, is a very long novel – about eight hundred pages. The story begins when Mr Allworthy discovers a baby boy has been placed in his bed one night. Allworthy is a kindly man, and he decides to adopt the mysterious child, giving it the name Tom Jones. He chooses the surname Jones because he assumes that the mother of the child is Jenny Jones, who is a servant of the schoolmaster Partridge.

Jenny Jones and Partridge are accused of being the parents of the child, and the evidence against them convinces Mr Allworthy. Partridge is dismissed from his job, and he and Jenny Jones leave the neighbourhood.

Mr Allworthy's sister, Bridget, marries an unpleasant man called Captain Blifil, and they have a son, Master Blifil, who is brought up with Tom. The two boys are educated by tutors, Thwackum and Square.

At the age of nineteen Tom has grown into a good-looking and generous young man. He becomes aware that he is falling in love with Squire Western's daughter, Sophia, but fights against the attraction because he knows that the squire wants his daughter to marry Master Blifil whose worldly expectations are greater than his own. He turns his attention to one of the gamekeeper's daughters, Molly Seagrim. She becomes pregnant, and Tom is

determined to be loyal to her. He discovers by chance that Molly
has had several lovers before him, and that he is not the father of
her child.

Tom is sent away by Mr Allworthy after Blifil manages to
persuade the kindly man that Tom has a bad character. Tom
leaves very sadly, and thinks of going to sea. On the road,
however, he falls in with some soldiers and decides to join the
army. This plan comes to nothing when he is involved in a fight
with an officer and injured.

The man who treats Tom for his wound is Partridge. They tell
each other their stories, and Partridge insists that he is not Tom's
father. They agree to travel together, and pass one night at the inn
at Upton. Here Tom has an affair with another guest at the inn,
Mrs Waters.

Sophia Western runs away from home to avoid being forced by
her father to marry Blifil. By chance she is staying at the same
inn at Upton and learns that Tom is spending the night with
another woman. She is very angry and leaves for London.

Tom and Partridge discover Sophia's notebook and some money
that she has left on the road, and they follow her to London. Here
Tom becomes involved with the society woman Lady Bellaston.
Sophia is a relative of Lady Bellaston, and is staying with her.
Tom breaks off the affair with Lady Bellaston but Sophia is again
angry with him.

Tom is arrested after a fight in which it appears he has killed a
man. In the end, however, he is released, and learns the truth
about his parentage. His father was a man called Summers who
had once stayed at Mr Allworthy's house, and his mother was Mr
Allworthy's sister, Bridget. Blifil had been entrusted with the
secret by his mother, but had kept the information to himself
instead of telling Mr Allworthy as Bridget had wished. Blifil is
now disgraced and Tom reinstated in the squire's affections. Tom
and Sophia are happily reunited.

2 Read the synopsis of *Tom Jones* carefully. What is wrong with the following statements?

a. Jenny Jones and Partridge leave the neighbourhood together.

b. Tom and Blifil are the same age.

c. When Mr Allworthy sends Tom away, Tom decides to join the army.

d. Partridge admits to Tom that he is his father.

e. The morning Sophia finds out that Tom has spent the night with Mrs Waters she tells him she never wants to see him again.

f. Blifil eventually tells Tom the truth about his (Tom's) parents.

3 We have seen how *Tom Jones* is a comic novel containing many misunderstandings. Can you remember some of them?

	Misunderstandings
Tom:	
Sophia:	

4 Fielding writes of Tom: 'Though he did not always act rightly, yet he never did it otherwise without feeling and suffering for it.'

a. Can you re-write this sentence in simpler English?

b. What are Tom's mistakes (women are always involved!) and how does he 'suffer' for these actions?

Tom's mistakes	The result

c. Tom often acted rightly in the story. Complete the list in chronological order of examples when Tom behaved rightly. The first and last have been done for you. Which event do you particularly approve of? Discuss your choice with your partner. Which is the most popular example in your class?

- In order to protect George Seagrim, Tom insisted he had been alone while shooting partridges on Squire Western's land.

- Tom forgives Blifil for what he has done.

Exercise 1 a– page 138

Mr Allworthy – A, E / Sophia – F, I, J / Partridge – B, H / Squire Western – J /
Jenny Jones/Mrs Waters – B, G / Mrs Western – F, J

Exercise 2 a– page 141

a. They leave separately.

b. Blifil is born later.

c. His first idea is to run away to sea.

d. No, he doesn't.

e. She doesn't meet him at Upton.

f. No, he doesn't (Mr Dowling reveals the truth).

Exercise 3 – page 141

	Misunderstandings
Tom:	• Tom thought he was the father of Molly's child. • Fitzpatrick thought he had entered his wife's bedroom at Upton. • At the inn at Upton, Squire Western sees Tom coming down stairs with Sophia's muff and assumes he had slept with his daughter. • Tom goes to Lady Bellaston's party and assumes the lady in the mask is a friend of Sophia's. • Tom thinks he has committed incest by sleeping with Mrs Waters. • Tom thinks he has murdered Fitzpatrick.
Sophia:	• Mrs Western believes Sophia is in love with Blifil. • Sophia is told of Tom's letter of proposal to Lady Bellaston.

Exercise 4 a – page 142

Tom didn't always behave well but he didn't deliberately want to harm other
people and he always felt sorry for what he did and suffered for his actions, too.

Exercise 4 b – page 142

Tom's mistakes	The result
Molly Seagrim (twice)	• Tom thinks he is the father of Molly's child; on the second occasion he is attacked by Blifil and Thwackum. Blifil uses the event to influence Allworthy's decision to send Tom away.
Mrs Waters	• Sophia finds out about Tom's night with Mrs Waters; Tom later fears he has committed incest.
Lady Bellaston	• She helps Lord Fellamar to wrongly accuse Tom in the incident with Fitzpatrick.

Exercise 3 c – page 142

- In order to protect George Seagrim, Tom insisted he had been alone while shooting partridges on Squire Western's land.
- Tom tried to save Sophia's bird and hurt himself as a result.
- Tom asked Sophia to persuade her father to give Black George a job.
- Tom admits immediately to being the father of Molly's child.
- Tom catches Sophia after falling from her horse. He breaks his arm as a result.
- Tom offers Molly money.
- Tom is genuinely happy about Allworthy's recovery.
- Tom defends Sophia's good name by calling Northerton a liar.
- Tom rescues Mrs Waters from Northerton.
- Tom, finding Sophia's money, is determined to return it to her.
- Tom convinces Nightingale to marry Nancy Miller.
- Tom forgives Blifil for what he has done.